DARIN,

It was such

a pleasure sharing

our personal journey

Enjoy life Always!

Tilt Shift Series: Abide is a work of fiction. Names, characters, places, and incidents either are the product of the author's imagination or are used fictitiously. Any resemblance to actual persons, living or dead, events, or locales is entirely coincidental.

ISBN: 9798359136839

The Williams family is no stranger to heartache and pain. Over the years they have experienced rape, death, betrayal, abandonment, and emotional pain beyond belief. Through the years, their hard times in life left them feeling like they were born into a Godless world and forced to live a Godforsaken life. While three siblings, Evelyn, Daniel, and Sabreena, have managed to rely on each other to get through the dysfunctional life that they've inherited, they can't help but to think that there will ever be a time of peace and happiness for them. As they face their most recent tragedy, their lives seem to be in the midst of a storm that they will never see themselves through. They will face times that they alone could never weather. As they journey through this storm together, each of them, individually, are in search of a peace so amazing that it could only be from God. But, who among them will come to the realization that, though their lives are unimaginably complicated, the God that they've searched for was never as far away from them as they thought?

Abide

*May these words of my mouth and this
meditation of my heart be pleasing in your
sight, Lord, my Rock and my Redeemer.
Psalm 19:14 NIV*

Evelyn

It was a dreary Saturday morning. The air held that all too familiar smell, you know-when the last days of summer are giving into the new fall season. It was raining hard, yet the sound of Evelyn weeping through purple, black, bruised eyes could be heard over the pounding of raindrops falling onto the porch awning, as well as the intermittent claps of thunder that permeated the atmosphere. Evelyn sat down beside his lifeless body. She still had the gun that put the sorry bastard out of his misery in her hand. She began to yell out through her bloody battered lips, "Are you happy now?!? Huh, you sick bastard! You sorry excuse for a man! You waste of a soul! I gave you everything, all of me, and you ripped my heart from its core just to watch it stop beating in the palm of your hand! Why!? Why couldn't you just love me the way that I loved you?"

She began sobbing uncontrollably as the reality of what just took place set in. She sat up and grabbed the bottle of vodka sitting next to her husband. It was the same bottle of poison that he was nearly through when he began pummeling on her like his own personal punching bag; the same poison that was always at the beginning of Evelyn's bad days. She cursed the bottle as she lifted it to her mouth. The first swig tinged the liquid in the bottle from the amount of blood still resting on her lips. She looked at it and sobbed even harder. Evelyn wasn't a drinker, she hated alcohol. It was behind the monstrous memories of her father before it eventually took him, it was slowly consuming the life of her only brother, and now it was the evil behind the abusive marriage that had suddenly found its violent end.

She continued to drink as she cursed the bottle's contents. "Unn Hmm, so you are the lord his god that unleashed him from the gates of hell?!? You are the evil spirit behind my bumps, cuts, and bruises?!? Ten years! Ten years I've loved, catered to, respected, submitted to, and remained faithful to this… this man, and for the last eight, all he did was worship you then beat up on me! I hope you both are happy!" Evelyn reached into her side table drawer and grabbed the bottle of sleeping pills she used to ease her to sleep many nights. She poured a handful into her mouth and washed them down with a swallow of vodka. Then she poured another handful and swallowed them down just like the first. She lied down next to her husband and grabbed his hand. With tears still trailing down the sides of her beaten face she turned to him and said, "I don't know why, but I forgive you. Til' death do us part." Evelyn then looked to the sky, with heart-filled bitterness and she spoke softly, "God, I don't remember a time in my life where I ever felt you existed. In all of my thirty-two years all I ever knew was pain and sorrow, so if you really exist and you can hear me ... show me." Evelyn closed her eyes and drifted, away from the pain, away from the sorrow, away from the loneliness, away from it all.

Sabreena

"Hey Ma, can u hand me my cell? I've been tryna reach my sister Eve all day. It ain't like her to not call me back after she sees that she missed my call." Sabreena's life partner Inez handed her the phone with an attitude and walked away. Sabreena took notice but was too concerned about Evelyn's whereabouts to speak on it at the time. She dialed Evelyn's phone for the eighth time that day; and still no answer. Sabreena left a message, "Hey Eve, its Bree. I'm worried about you sissy. Please call me back. You know how I feel about Troy, so pleeease don't make me call his phone. Okay? I love you; talk to you soon." Sabreena tossed the phone on the bed and rushed to see what Inez's problem was.

"Umm, you wanna tell me what that was all about?" Sabreena asked. Inez cut her eyes over at Sabreena and began explaining, "Look Bree, we've been in a committed relationship for six months now. We've been friends for over thirteen years. I know you said you wanted to wait until we had our ceremony to be intimate, but I'm beginning to think that the ceremony is never going to happen." Inez continued, "Bree, you ever consider the fact that maybe you're not gay at all?" With a puzzled look on her face Bree responded, "Umm, no! Why would you even think that Inez? I love you; you know that. Where is all of this coming from anyway?" Inez patted her lap for Sabreena to come and sit down. She knew that what she was about to say would open up pandora's box, but it had to be said. Inez attempting to tread carefully responded, "Listen Bree, you know I love you to, but I'm starting to think that maybe you should talk to someone about your past. Sweetie, I think you keep me around because you are afraid of men, but you don't want to be lonely. You've never even been with a woman before this, or anyone else now that I think about it." Inez continues, "I think that when your uncle raped you, you never got the help or the closure you needed. I mean, your dad was a drunk, and he just drowned himself in a bottle after it happened. When he was sober, he blamed your mom for allowing it to happen and then used it as a reason to just go out and drink again. Need I even start on your brother, and how he picked up the bottle right after that happened? Daniel can't even look at you in the eye til' this day, and he refuses to get involved with anyone because he fears that he will fail to protect them. The two of you were so close and he blames himself for not being able to protect you that night; and I'm not even gonna address your sister Eve and her crazy, alcoholic husband. All of you were affected in some way by what happened, and I think that you "deciding" that you are gay may be how you are coping with avoiding men, but not being alone."

Sabreena sat quietly for a while in deep thought. "Sabreena?" Inez said softly as she turned Bree's face to look at hers and held it between her hands, "I know my timing is horrible, but I have to do this now. I can't stand between you and life anymore. I will always love you, but I need you to let me go. I can tell by the way that you tense up every time I touch you in an intimate way that you are not comfortable with this. I know you love me, but who doesn't love a person that has been a true friend for as long as we have been friends. Besides, did you think I forgot how much of a "church girl" you were before he-." "SHUT UP!" Sabreena interrupted, "Shut-up! Don't say it again! You made your point! Look, I gotta find my sister. I ain't got time for this, so if you're leaving, then get out! Spare me the dramatic exit Inez!" "But Bre-". Sabreena held her hand up to stop her mid-sentence. She was done with the conversation. She hopped up off of Inez's lap and left her sitting dumb founded in the chair. As Sabreena went back upstairs to retrieve her phone she shouted from a distance, "And do me a favor, when you get to wherever you're going, forget you ever knew me!"

Sabreena sat on the edge of her bed and dialed her brother, Daniel's number hoping that he could find his way out of the bottle and to his phone. That didn't happen so she just left him a voice mail. "Hey D, this is baby sis. I haven't heard from Eve all day and I'm getting worried. You live closer so I thought maybe you could go check on her. Gimme a call back when you get this message or if you hear from her, Okay? I love you bro, bye." Sabreena hung up the phone and laid down. She crossed her hands over her belly and before she closed her eyes, she thought of doing something she hadn't done for years. She began to speak out loud, "God, I'm worried about my sister. If you could just give me a sign that—Man, who am I kidding...There is no God". Sabreena rolled over and shut her eyes. "Uggh, so over this day!" she said bitterly as she drifted off to sleep.

Daniel

Daniel sat at the bar staring at himself in a mirror that seemed as if it was strategically placed behind the bar to give a person a wide angled view of their guilty pleasure. He stared at himself with thoughts of pure self-disgust. He began to drift back in time in his mind. His thoughts took him back to that dreadful evening that changed his whole life. ~ "Mom, Bree, Eve, anybody home?" A young and vibrant Daniel stopped in the kitchen like he did every time he came in from playing basketball. He opened the fridge, grabbed and opened the carton of orange juice, placed it to his mouth, and began gulping straight from the carton. As he drank, he thought he could hear the distant sounds of his little sister sobbing. "Bree, is that you?" Daniel put the orange juice back and started up the back stair well. He came closer to the sound as he made his way to his younger sister's room. The door was cracked, and he peeked in just enough to see Sabreena holding the covers up to her neck. She was crying and gasping, and she had a look of intense fear on her face. "What the - - Bree, what's wrong? Daniel asked as he pushed the door open. Sabreena was in shock, she couldn't speak. All she could do was gaze and cry.

Daniel approached her quickly to console her, but as he got closer Sabreena's eyes grew wider and she let out an ear-piercing yelp! Before Daniel could turn around, he was struck in the head from behind and knocked out.

When Daniel came to, his vision was blurry, and he struggled to sit up. He suddenly remembered the look of terror on Sabreena's face right before he was struck. He jumped to his feet only to find Sabreena laying in her bed in a daze. Her night gown was smeared with blood from the waist down and she trembled intensely. "Oh God! Sabreena! Oh God, please... Sabreena, please be ok!" Daniel ran and grabbed the phone from his mother's room. He dialed 911 and ran back to his sister's side. Never hanging up the phone after calling for help, he dropped the phone and swooped Sabreena up into his arms. He ran with her in his arms, down the stairs and out of the front door. "Help! Help us please! Somebody please, help us!" The sound of sirens approaching, and the flashing of red and blue lights slowly faded as Daniel came back to his present mind. There he sat, in the bar with tears trailing his grief filled face. The barmaid startled him with questions of concern. "Yo D - you aight?"

Coming completely out of his haunting memories, Daniel answered, "Yeah, I'm good. Hey, can I clear my tab? I gotta get outta here."

Daniel paid the bar maid and reached into his pocket for his cell as he left the bar. "Dang, I missed Bree's call" he said as he dialed her back. "Hello, Bree? You called?" Bree responded half asleep and out of it, "Yeah, you hear from sissy today? I haven't been able to reach her all day and that's not like her." Daniel, now worried as well, responded, "Naw, but I'm around the corner from her house. Did you call Troy?" Bree snapped back, "Now you know I can't stand dude! I ain't callin' his phone!" Daniel turned the corner of Evelyn's street and told Sabreena, "aight, I'm on the block now. Imma call you back when I get with Eve."

Daniel hung up the phone just as he was walking up Evelyn's front steps. He began to ring the bell and bang on the door. "Eve! Eve, open up! It's D! Eve I gotta use the bathroom! Eve!" Daniel yelled. He knew she was in there because her car was parked out front. He walked around to the side of the house but couldn't see anything. It was seven in the evening and now dark, so he wondered why there were no lights on in the house. He went around to the back of the house and found the window to the half bathroom cracked open. He poked a hole in the screen with his keys and then ripped it open. "Awe man, my sister is gonna kill me for this" Daniel said under his breath as he climbed into the window. "Eve it's D, I'm coming up yo!" Daniel was yelling as he made his way up the stairs so he wouldn't catch Evelyn off guard.

He reached the top of the stairs, turned the corner and approached the master bedroom. As he got closer, he felt a rush. Were his eyes deceiving him? It can't be, he thought. "Oh my God; Troy, Eve! God please, not again!" Daniel quickly rushed over to Troy's cold, bloody, lifeless body. Then he ran around the other side to find Evelyn lying still, barely breathing; her pulse was almost non-existent. He pulled out his cell phone and dialed 911. "Hello, please hurry! I need help at 1232 Meade Street! My brother-in-law has been shot and my sister is not breathing!" Daniel dropped the phone and began doing CPR on Evelyn. With every breath that he gave his sister, he got a deep sinking feeling in the bottom of his gut. He began to cry at the thought of losing her. He could hear the sirens in the distance. His thoughts of the past and his present fiasco began to collide in his mind. Daniel suddenly heard banging at the front door. He picked up his phone, scurried down the hall and down the stairs to let the Paramedics in. He directed them to the master bedroom. Still in shock and in total disbelief, Daniel collapsed to his knees as the medics rushed pass him and up the stairs. Full of rage and pain Daniel bellowed, "Where are you! My God, where are you when we need you! If you are real, then why have you always turned your back on us!"

Daniel's phone started vibrating in his hand. Still in a haze, he looked at his phone to see who was calling. It was Sabreena; Daniel had never called her back. With a blank stare, Daniel held the phone in his hand wondering how he could even begin to tell his sister what was happening. The phone stopped vibrating momentarily then it began again. He answered the call. "Bree", Daniel said softly as tears fell rapidly and silently to the floor, "Bree, I was too late. I, I was too late Bree. I'm sorry Bree, I was too late. I'm always too late Bree. I'm so sorry. I'm so sorry." Daniel dropped the phone and began to sob hysterically as a panic-stricken Sabreena

yelled through the phone wanting to know
what godforsaken tragedy could they
possibly be facing now.

Psalm 40:12

For troubles without number
surround me; my sins have overtaken me,
and I cannot see. They are more than the
hairs of my head, and my heart fails within
me.

Daniel and Sabreena spent the better
part of the last three months at St. Mary's
hospital, sitting restlessly at Evelyn's side;
hoping that each day would be different
from the day before. Evelyn's condition
hadn't gotten any better since she was
stabilized. She was still in a coma and was
not showing any signs of regaining
consciousness. She was still attached to life
support and the once annoying clicking
sound of the machine that breathed life into
her had grown to be the only comforting
sound that adorned her solemn condition.
Evelyn's care, since being admitted, had
been managed by Dr. Cole, who had been
her Dr. for the last twelve years. After
completing his visit with Evelyn on the
anniversary of her third month since she was
admitted, Dr. Cole thought that it was time
to discuss Evelyn's lack of progress and
how to move forward, with the family.

Daniel and Sabreena held hands
while sitting across the table from Dr. Cole

in the small conference room. As he made his best attempt to explain to them as plainly as possible, the severity of Evelyn's condition and the odds of her ever regaining her consciousness, you could almost see the hope exit through their weeping eyes as they digested the news. The thought of the hospital expenses, the chance that Evelyn would probably never be the same if she ever was to wake up, the charges that she faced for her husband's death if she was mentally intact when she awoke; it was all too much to deal with and sort through so suddenly. "I can't do this! I'm sorry Bree—Dr. Cole, I need to excuse myself. I'm sorry." Daniel said abruptly as he turned Sabreena's hand loose and left the conference room.

Sabreena sat at the table in awkward silence for about a minute, then she apologized for her brother's sudden pardoning. "Dr. Cole, I-we will get back to you with a decision tomorrow. All things considered, I think the decision has made itself; we just need some time to wrap our heads around this and say goodbye. Thank you for everything, but I need to go now." Sabreena left the conference room and swiftly began making her way to Evelyn's room where she was sure she would find

Daniel. As she approached her sister's hospital room, she could see someone standing over Evelyn, holding her hand and planting a kiss on her forehead. She cleared her throat as she entered the room to get the attention of the visitor. "Umm, hello" Sabreena said softly as she approached, but when the woman turned around Sabreena stopped dead in her tracks. She began to tremble, and she lost color in her face as if she had seen a ghost.

Sabreena stared at the woman and felt as if she was looking in a mirror, only at the reflection of an older and more sophisticated version of herself. She took a step back and clutched her chest. She opened her mouth to speak but nothing would come out. So, the woman decided to speak first to ease the tense moment. "Hey baby girl, you turned out to be even more beautiful than I had imagined." Sabreena's mother said coyly, not knowing exactly how Sabreena would respond to her mere presence. "What are you—how did you— what...?", Sabreena fumbled over her words. She hadn't seen her mother since her father passed away eight years ago. She couldn't even begin to sort her feelings. She didn't know if she wanted to be angry, relieved, bitter, sad, happy, or just plain indifferent.

Sabreena finally snapped back, "Where did you come from and how did you find out about Eve?!?" Her mother attempted to approach her as she answered, "Eve always knew how to reach me, but it's complicated, Bree. Can we do this somewhere else?" Sabreena stepped back again and retorted, "No. Here is just as good a place as anywhere; and what do you mean Eve knew how to reach you? And what does that have to do with how you found Eve here? She's been in a coma for three months Marie!"

Noticing the level of Sabreena's discomfort as well as how angry she was, Marie stepped back before answering, "Marie? Wow, you've never called me by my name before. I guess I deserve that." Marie found her way to a chair before beginning to explain, "Bree, I was severely depressed after you were"—Marie stopped abruptly. She still couldn't even fix her lips to say it. Sabreena stared with intensity waiting for her mother to explain. Marie continued, "I couldn't believe that something so horrible could happen to anyone I knew, let alone my own child. I felt like I had failed you and that you would never forgive me. I couldn't turn to your father to help me put our lives back together and I didn't know how to help you. And I know this might sound crazy, but him constantly blaming me and hating me actually made me feel like I was getting some type of deserved punishment for failing you. After he died, I was left with my guilt of leaving you home alone that night and no one to constantly remind me. I couldn't even get you help because you refused to talk about it to anyone, and you lashed out every time we tried to force you to accept help. Eve was old enough to take care of you and D so I"—Sabreena interrupted, "Let me stop you, because I remember this part so well MARIE! You skipped cooking up the stew and just stepped!"

Marie sat quietly with her head down before responding. She looked back up at Sabreena and continued, "It wasn't like that, and I don't expect you to understand Bree; but I felt defeated, and I was no good to any of you. Eve was so strong, and I knew she would take good care of you two. I sat her down and explained everything to her. She never even hesitated to step up. I cashed out your father's life insurance policy and put it in the bank. I sent checks every month to a safe deposit box so that Evelyn could cover the expense of caring for the two of you. I checked myself into a hospital to get the help I needed to get through what I was feeling. I figured that I would never be of any use to my children if I didn't get help." Marie paused to gauge Sabreena's reaction to what was being said. When she realized that Sabreena was becoming receptive, she continued, "I spent a full year, getting treatment for my depression and another year learning to help other women who came through the program. It was shortly after being gone for two years that I learned that I had stage three, ovarian cancer". Sabreena's eyes widened with concern. Marie knew just from the look in her daughter's eyes that she didn't hate her.

Marie slid her chair closer to Sabreena who was now sitting across from her. She began to speak again, "I met with Eve and told her that I was ill and together, we decided that you and D were doing too well for us to shake up things by me coming back sick; especially since we didn't know whether I would live or die. You were about to start your junior year in high school and D was about to start his senior year. I honestly thought that I had made a decision that was best for you two and even though it was harder for me than when I decided to leave, I figured that I at least owed you and your brother that much. By the time you graduated from high school, my cancer had been in full remission for almost two years. I wanted to come back into your lives then, but I was afraid to take that step. I put it off and kept creating what would be the perfect time in my mind. A month ago, I found out that my cancer has come out of remission, and I just told myself that this day would never come and that I would die before ever reconnecting with you and D."

Sabreena began to cry silently. Marie reached out for her hand and Sabreena kindly obliged. As Marie held on to her daughter's hand for the first time in years, tears began to roll down her face as well. She spoke through teary eyes and a shaky voice, "I am truly sorry Sabreena, God knows I am. I have always lived my life for my children. Since the first time I laid eyes on Eve, I knew that she and any children I had after her would be the center of my world and the reason behind my very existence. Sabreena must have had me listed as her next of kin, and when I got the call from Dr. Cole about what happened I nearly died where I stood. I've called every day since then; but when I talked to Dr. Cole today, he informed me that I had to make a decision and that he would speak to you and D when you arrived today. I don't blame either of you if you never forgive me, but I could not let the two of you face this time alone. I refused to fail any of you again." Sabreena clinched her mother's hand tightly and cried harder as she began to respond, "Mommy, I can't let her go. I'm not ready. I still need her here. I just can't do it." Marie got up out of her chair and pulled Sabreena up with her. She wrapped her arms tightly around her daughter and said, "Baby girl, I know this is hard. But when God says it's time, it ain't much we gonna be able to do but pray for the strength to make it through this time. Ain't nothing more unnatural than having your child leave this earth before you, but I've learned that God has good reasoning for everything He allows us to live through. Now I've been praying for the Lord to find it in His will to let my baby come out of this, but now it's time for us to pray on what He'll have us do now.

Sabreena pushed away from her mother angrily. Marie, now confused asked, "Bree, what's wrong sweetie?" Sabreena aggressively wiped the tears away from her eyes and shot a daggering look in her mother's direction and said, "How could you sit here and talk about a god that never shows up for us mom. Do you even hear yourself! Look at us! Look at Eve laying there totally helpless! Look at me! And you have to live with cancer…TWICE!" Completely floored by Sabreena's outburst, Marie attempts to carefully respond to her daughter saying, "Baby girl, I don't think you mean that. You're just angry right now. Please, just"— "No!" Sabreena yelled back, "No, I won't pray! Why should I! I never did anything to deserve any of this, yet He never stopped it! He never does: and you know why mommy?!? Because He doesn't exist! I'm sorry but that's how I truly feel! So, how bout I leave you to waste your own time praying to your worthless God! I gotta get outta here. This is all too much for me right now."

Sabreena gathered her things as Marie's thoughts scattered to think of what to say. As Sabreena approached the doorway Marie said, "Bree, you can't leave now, Eve needs us here." Sabreena turned and looked at her mother and coldly retorted, "Oh but I can mother, guess we have more in common than I actually thought!" Sabreena rolled her eyes, turned and proceeded to walk out of the door. Just as she was approaching the elevator, the doors opened, and Daniel stepped out. In an apologetic tone, he says to Sabreena, "Hey sis, I'm sorry for cutting out on you like that. It's just that"-- Sabreena stuck her hand up for him to stop talking and then interrupted, "Save it, no need to be sorry. Apparently, we got it honest. Don't even sweat it." Sabreena stepped on to the elevator and left Daniel standing there with a confused look on his face. Before the doors closed, she called out with a smug smirk on her face, "Oh, and D... have fun." "Smooches", Sabreena sang as the doors shut completely.

Daniel, now totally confused and shaking his head as he walked back to Evelyn's hospital room mumbled under his breath, "What the heck was that about?" Daniel cut the corner to the hall that led to Evelyn's room completely clueless as to what he would find when he got there. As he got closer, he heard a familiar voice. Marie was praying and crying out loud about the condition that her family was in. Daniel reached the doorway and could not believe his eyes. He stopped in his tracks and blurted out, "You have GOT to be kidding me!" Marie, startled, abruptly stopped praying and looked her only son in the face. For a solid thirty seconds the two of them stared at each other in silence, then Marie parted her lips and mouthed the words, "God, help us", then she burst into tears.

Daniel remained silent and appeared to be unmoved by Marie's sobbing. He stood emotionless, staring at Marie like a deer caught in headlights. Not knowing what to say, what to do, or even how to feel; he turned to leave. "Daniel!" Marie shouted as he began to exit. Daniel stopped and turned to look at Marie. She began to plead with Daniel, "Daniel please, don't go. I can't begin to tell you how sorry I am. I know my apology can never make up for the choices that I've made, but D...it's all I've got. I have no right to ask you this, but please...please stay?" Daniel, still silent and emotionally conflicted inside, slowly made his way into the room and sat down.

The two of them sat in awkward silence for a while; both of them not knowing how to express what they were feeling at that very moment. Marie, not wanting to risk him throwing a fit and leaving the same way that Sabreena had done, decided to turn to Evelyn's bedside and hold her hand as she prayed aloud, *"Lord, if we ever needed you before; we absolutely need you to get through these trying times right now. Dear God, I come*

to you battered, broken, helpless, and
defeated. My family has been torn apart
and we have suffered trials and tribulations
unimaginable to others. But your word
Lord...your word says that you will never
leave of forsake us, Lord. Your word says
that if we ask, that it will be given. So,
Lord, I come to you in faith, and ask that
you have mercy on us this day. I pray that
you will take up our burdens and lighten
our loads. Please, give us the wisdom to
abide by accept your will, and give us the
strength to forgive and mend what is
broken between us so that we may stand
strong together. In Jesus name I Pray.
Amen."

As Marie lifted her head and turned
to face Daniel once again, her heart sank as
she was faced with an empty chair. In the
midst of her being consumed in prayer, and
without him making a sound, Daniel had
made the decision to leave Marie on her
own.

Matthew 24:36

"But about that day or hour no one knows, not even the angels in heaven, nor the Son, but only the Father.

Daniel and Sabreena comforted each other as they stood beside Evelyn's hospital bed, saying goodbye to the one person they felt they could always count on. Marie, being listed as Evelyn's only next of kin, had made the decision to pull the plug and remove Evelyn from life support. Even though Sabreena knew in her heart of hearts that she and Daniel would have made the same decision, in some selfish way it made her feel better to be angry at Marie for making this decision. Sabreena cried as she held on to Daniel for support. She pouted as she spoke, "It's just not right D. How does she get to disappear when it's convenient for her, then come back into our lives and make a decision that rips away the only person who has ever been there for us?!? How could she D? We gotta do something; we can't just give up on Eve!"

Daniel held on to Sabreena, trying to be strong for her and putting his grief aside. He turned Sabreena to face him and for the first time in years, he looked her in her eyes. Daniel spoke sternly to Sabreena saying,

"Bree, I know this is the hardest thing that
we have ever had to do. I don't know how,
but just like every other time, we're gonna
get through this. We have to be strong Bree.
Eve would want us to be. And who knows,
but if there is a God maybe he will allow
Eve to be our guardian angel and continue to
look after us." Daniel felt foolish just
saying that, but he wanted to find the words
to console Bree and give him-self comfort in
the process. Daniel continued, "Man, I
don't know. I'm lost without her Bree, but I
have to believe that we can get through this,
and this time around I'm gonna be here for
you. I'm never gonna fail you again.
Believe that."

Daniel wiped the tears from
Sabreena's face and they both turned and
held on to different parts of Evelyn to say
goodbye. Sabreena felt a warm rush and
then was overcome with that strange feeling
she used to get when she was a little girl at
church, during praise and worship. She
looked up at Daniel and said, "D, did you
really mean what you just said... you know,
about Sabreena being a guardian angel and
all?" Daniel smiled at Sabreena and said,
"Yes baby sis, every word." Daniel knew
his little sister all too well and could see the
thoughts brewing in her head. "What is it,

Bree? Just say it." Daniel said as he studied her expressions. Bree, with a calming look on her face, grabbed Daniel by the hand and said, "D, I think I—Umm, I think I want to say a prayer for Eve. You know, just in case." Daniel, playing coy, says, "just in case what?" Sabreena, now annoyed by his question snapped back, "Seriously D. Just bow your head!" Sabreena closed her eyes and began to pray, "*Lord, if you are there, please forgive my sister for her sins and welcome her into your kingdom with open arms. Oh yeah, and if it's possible, please allow her to check on me and D—and even mommy, every once in a while. Thanks. Amen*". Daniel and Sabreena, still holding hands, said their final goodbyes to Evelyn.

They, as well as Marie, had chosen not to be present when the doctor took Evelyn off of the machines. As they left the hospital room, they informed the staff that no one would be back and that they were free to carry out the orders to pull the plug from their beloved sister. Marie had agreed to allow Daniel and Sabreena handle the funeral arrangements, especially since she was so far removed from her children's lives for the past eight years. So, after leaving the hospital they decided not to drag things along, and they went directly to the funeral home to make the arrangements for Evelyn's home going service.

As Daniel and Sabreena drove to their destination, they began to talk about what it was like growing up with Evelyn after their mother left. They laughed through tears as the melancholy emotions took hold of them. Sabreena began to think about how close she and her brother used to be and how they drifted over the years. She wished that they could be that close again, but then the thought of watching Daniel drink himself to death quickly pushed those thoughts away. Sabreena's mood changed suddenly as she struggled with the thought of losing Daniel and being alone, without either of her siblings. Then her thoughts shifted again, and she tried to think of the last time that she even smelled a hint of alcohol coming from Daniel since finding Evelyn that night, three months ago.

"Oh My Goodness!" Sabreena blurted out. Daniel slammed on his breaks, as Sabreena's sudden outburst startled him. Daniel looked over at Sabreena and yells, "What the heck Sabreena! Are you tryna get us both killed?" Sabreena overwhelmed with happiness, slapped her brother on the arm playfully and said, "I'm sorry D. Didn't mean to scare you, I just thought about something. When was the last time you had a drink?" Daniel, now wearing a frown, continued driving as he answered Sabreena, "I didn't think anyone noticed. I haven't had a drink since I left the bar on the night that I found Eve and Troy. It was stupid, but I kinda got this crazy idea that if there was a God, that I would give up drinking and try to do everything right in my life, if He would let Eve live. So much for that deal though, huh? Guess it was just wishful thinking."

Sabreena, now sad again, turned to her brother and let out a very quiet, "Oh." Daniel sensed her disappointment and said, "Bree, I meant what I said about not failing you ever again, and that includes me staying sober. I miss the way we used to be. You're my baby sister, and we only have each other now. Not having Eve here to stay on my case about every little thing I do wrong has forced me to take a good look at myself. I understand now, just how much I haven't been there for you, and I can't take that time back so for that I'm sorry. I have made the decision to change for both your sake and mine. Believe me Bree, things are gonna be different from now on. Big bro is gonna get on your last nerve! Now cheer up ya big baby, 'cause you ain't getting rid of me no time soon."

Sabreena smiled as she looked at her big brother and felt like she was looking into the face of the big brother she once admired so much. "I love you, Daniel." Sabreena said happily. Daniel now pulling into a parking space, put the car into park and said, "Ditto squirt" then yanked Sabreena's nose like he used to do when they were kids. The two of them exited the car and approached the funeral home hand in hand to complete a task that neither of them ever imagined that they would ever have to complete. Just as they were entering the funeral home, Sabreena's cell phone rang. She pulled out her phone to look at the number, "It's that number that mommy has been calling us from. I hope she didn't change her mind about us handling the arrangements. As a matter of fact, I'm not gonna answer. I'll get back to her later." Sabreena said sounding annoyed. She then sent the call to her voicemail and she and Daniel proceeded to handle their business of burying their sister.

Job 5:9

*He performs wonders that cannot
be fathomed, miracles that cannot be
counted.*

During the ride home, Daniel and
Sabreena both admitted to feeling a bit
relieved that they were putting the everyday
anxiety of the possibility of Evelyn's
condition changing or the disappointment of
things not changing, behind them. It had
been a very stressful three months, filled
with as many hopeful days as discouraging
ones. Sabreena, still annoyed by the fact
that Marie called her repeatedly while they
were making the home going arrangements,
began to fuss; "Why the heck is she still
calling me? Leave a message already!
Geesh, I just don't have the energy to deal
with her today!"

Daniel, who was a little more
easygoing than Sabreena, made light of the
situation. "Awe cut it out Bree. Don't be
that way. Before, you complained that she
never wrote or at least called, so be happy
that she's blowing up your cell now. Guess
you gotta be careful what you ask for", D
said jokingly. Sabreena rolled her eyes and
crossed her arms as she retorted, "ha ha…
you gotz jokes. Whatever! Easy for you to

say, you didn't give her your number. At
least she left a message this time. Now let
me see what on earth was soooo important,
that "mommy dearest" just couldn't wait
until I got back to her to tell me.

Sabreena dialed her voice mail and
listened to the message Marie left. She
immediately dropped her cell phone and
began crying hysterically. Daniel, startled
and confused, swiftly pulled the car over and
began trying to console Sabreena. "Bree, its
ok, its ok. I know this is tough, but we're
gonna get through this. Please, just calm
down. Sissy wouldn't want you making
such a big fuss over her" Daniel said as he
leaned over and held Sabreena trying to
calm her. But nothing Daniel said brought
her out of her hysterical state.

Sabreena gasped in between crying.
Eyes wide open as if she was trying to speak
but couldn't get it out. Finally, in between
gasps, she squeezed out; "Oh my God D!"
Daniel was growing anxious as he held her
shoulders in his hands, now waiting for her
to say something more. In frustration, he
gave her a shake and yelled, "Bree, what is
it? You are scaring me! Is mommy ok?"
But Sabreena still couldn't get it out. She
just continued to weep with no control.

Daniel, now feeling helpless and frustrated, hopped out of the car and ran around to Sabreena's door. He opened it and reached for her phone that had fallen to the floor. He dialed his mother's phone number from the list of missed calls as he got back into the car. "Mom, please answer!" Daniel said through clinched teeth as the phone rang repeatedly. Just as Daniel thought he was going to lose it, Marie picked up, "Sabreena!" Marie yelled into the phone. "No, Mom it's me, Daniel! What's going on? I can't calm Sabreena down. Are you ok? Somebody tell me something before I lose it! Hello mom, you there?" Daniel spat on in a panic.

Marie was trying her best to calm her own self down before she answered. As she cried, she said to Daniel, "D, please, just come get me baby. We have to get over to the hospital. Oh, sweet Jesus! D, baby you ain't gon' believe this, but as sure as you can hear me speaking right now, there is a God! Oh, Sweet Jesus, Precious Lawd!" Marie was going on and on in a praise and Daniel was now confused and frustrated with both his mother and his sister. "Mommy!" Daniel yelled through the phone. "Mom, I can't drive like this. Now somebody is gonna have to tell me what the HECK is

goin' on before I go anywhere!" Daniel
demanded.

Marie, still in the midst of her praise,
said to Daniel, "Oh Glory be to God D! It's
your sister. Eve woke up D! Oh, praise
god, she woke up!" "Wha, What!" Daniel
said under his breath as the news took his
breath away with the force of a violent fall.
He hung up the phone and looked over at a
still hysterical Sabreena, but now
understanding her uncontrollable state.
Daniel began to cry silently. He sat in total
disbelief. He was so full of mixed emotions
that he couldn't compose himself to drive
right away.

"Ok, ok", Daniel said as he
attempted to sort through his thoughts and
regain control over his emotions. He
couldn't contain it anymore. He opened his
door and jumped up out of his car. Leaving
the door open behind him, he began to run
up and down the street full speed like a
maniac, yelling at the top of his lungs and
crying tears of joy. When he finally felt like
he had gotten himself under control, he
returned to his car and a now calm, but still
crying Sabreena.

Daniel and Sabreena, both
overwhelmed with happiness clinched each

other tight and cried in each other's arms until they both could cry no more. "Bro, I need to see her. I can't wait. We need to go now! Stuff like this just don't happen to us. Please D, let's go now!" Sabreena said frantically. "I know Bree, but we're closer to mommy, so can we just get her real quick then get over to the hospital?" Daniel pleaded. Sabreena slammed her fist down on the dashboard causing Daniel to jump nearly out of his skin and yelled, "NO! I'm not thinkin' 'bout Marie right now D! Take me to sissy now! You can go back for mommy."

Before Daniel could say anything back, Sabreena began to cry again. Apologetically she looked over at Daniel and said, "Bro I'm sorry, I just-I'm feeling crazy inside. Like I'm dreaming or something, but I know I'm not. I'm scared that I'm gon' wake up and this was just a dream, and that I was right for feelin' like good stuff like this just doesn't happen to us! I just need to lay my eyes on her long enough to know that this is real."

Sabreena, now realizing that they had already pulled up to their mother's house, decided to make an honest attempt to calm down, and just be patient. Daniel put the car into park and rubbed his forehead out of exhaustion. He said in an endearing tone, "Bree, this has been an eventful day for all of us; but you're going to have to try really hard to keep your "Steel Magnolias" emotions under control, 'cause I have a headache the size of China, so I'm not against slapping you silly right about now." Daniel couldn't hold a straight face any longer and he and Sabreena busted out laughing.

"I'm sorry baby sis, but it was getting too intense up in here. I had to lighten things up a bit" Daniel said to Sabreena playfully. Sabreena smiled at her big brother, appreciating his lighthearted spirit. Then in her sassy tone she said, "yeah, 'cause I was about to say, don't make me pull a Madea and go in my purse on you; crazy self, talkin' bout slapping somebody." Sabreena said as she shook her head and laughed again. As they got out of the car, Sabreena grabbed Daniel by the wrist and pulled him to her so she could hug on his arm, "Seriously Bro, I don't know what I would do without you right now"

Daniel, now feeling as if somehow, he had redeemed himself, smiled at his little sister, and just like he always used to do, he pinched her nose again and said, "Ditto squirt". Just then, Marie opened the door and Daniel extended his empty arm to his mother to help her down the steps. With his mother on one arm and his baby sister still clinging to the other arm, Daniel felt like his position in life had been restored. He knew that their lives were just beginning to change in many ways, and very suddenly, but he didn't back down at the thought of being the rock for the most important women in his life.

As he shut the car door for his mother, he looked up at the sky. It seemed as if the sun was shining just for him and only in his direction. He continued to look upward as he walked around his car. He paused at the rear of the car, and he could feel a strange warmth coming from the sun. It was almost as if someone bigger had wrapped their arms around him. It was at that moment that Daniel knew...Daniel smiled and mouthed the words, "Thank You" before lowering his head and continuing to walk. As he sat down to drive, a settling peace came over him; and Daniel was sure that his family was not alone in this.

James 1:2-4

Consider it pure joy, my brothers and sisters, whenever you face trials of many kinds, because you know that the testing of your faith produces perseverance. Let perseverance finish its work so that you may be mature and complete, not lacking anything.

"Hi. I need the room number for Evelyn Williams-Roberts please." Sabreena asked the women sitting behind the information desk. Daniel, noticing the confused look on the woman's face, felt a need to explain. He figured she was confused since they had been coming there for the last three months and needed no assistance finding their sister's room. "Oh, my sister is no longer in a coma, and she was moved to a different unit. That's why we need the room number now." Daniel explained. The woman smiled as she looked up their desired information. "She's been moved to room 634" the woman said politely. The family thanked her and proceeded to the elevators.

They were all so elated at the recent change in Evelyn's health status, that no one from the outside looking in would ever be able to tell that they had such unresolved issues. The three of them laughed as Sabreena told Marie about how Daniel ran up and down the street screaming like a maniac, and how he had threatened to slap her silly. They exited the elevator and made their way to Evelyn's room but were intercepted by Dr. Cole once they reached the nurse's station. "Hi, Mrs. Williams, Daniel, Sabreena; I know you all are anxious to get to Evelyn's room and lay eyes on her, but I need you to come with me to the family conference room while I catch you up on a few things." Dr. Cole pleasantly pronounced as he motioned for the family to follow.

Marie and Daniel kindly obliged, but Sabreena was not letting anything stop her from seeing Evelyn before she did anything else. No one even noticed that she had gone in the direction of Evelyn's hospital room instead of following Dr. Cole, but that lack of knowledge was short lived. "WHAT THE H-E- DOUBLE BENDY STRAWS IS THIS!!" Sabreena belted out, clearly infuriated by what she was seeing. Dr. Cole turned abruptly with a look of astonishment on his face, as he noticed that Sabreena had not followed them, and he quickly did the math. In that instance, it seemed as if the whole hospital floor had stopped moving.

Dr. Cole sped past Marie and Daniel, attempting to get to Sabreena before the inevitable took place. As Sabreena continued to raise Cain, Dr. Cole, Daniel and Marie couldn't get to the room fast enough. They all reached the room simultaneously and found Sabreena yelling at the two uniformed officers while tugging at the handcuffs that adorned one of Evelyn's arms and imprisoned her to the bedrail. "I mean it, I want them off now! This is crazy! My sister is not a criminal, and she's been through enough without you people treating her this way. Take 'em off!" Sabreena yelled desperately. "I'm sorry officers. Please forgive my sister. This just caught us by surprise." Daniel said apologetically as he grabbed Sabreena and forcefully removed her from the room. The three of them silently, but expeditiously followed Dr. Cole to the conference room and just as fast as the door closed behind them, Sabreena tore into Dr. Cole.

"You called the police! How can you even look us in the eye after betraying us this way! You cold hearted snitch! I can't believe the stones on you!" Sabreena yelled as she stood over Dr. Cole, refusing to sit. Dr. Cole, along with Daniel and Marie, sat seemingly unfazed by Sabreena's eruption, as this had become the norm for her. "And I thought you said she was awake. She looked comatose to me doc! The only thing that was missing was that dreadful clicking machine! Well, are you gonna say something or are you just gon' sit there with that stupid look on your face?" Sabreena spat sarcastically.

Dr. Cole sat quietly for a moment just to be sure that Sabreena was over her emotional fit. He then began to explain, "I asked that you all come and talk with me for this very reason. As I intended to explain before you entered Evelyn's room, I had to follow proper procedure and inform the detectives of Evelyn's waking as I was instructed. Now I am fully aware of everything this family has been through since this tragedy occurred. I have known Evelyn for many years and believe me when I tell you that calling that detective was one of the hardest things that I've had to do in my whole career." Dr. Cole lifted an eyebrow at Sabreena as she folded her arms and attempted to interject.

After seeing that she thought better of it, Dr. Cole continued, "to address the latter, Evelyn is heavily sedated because she was extremely, but understandably, combative when she woke up from her coma. We are planning to slowly bring her out of her sedation and at that time we will attempt to help her make heads or tails of her current situation. Your presence and your calm approach will be very much needed as we ease her through the long healing and physical therapy process. Her body has not been in a physically active state for quite some time, and she has a long road of recovery ahead of her. We will offer her psychiatric counseling to deal with the psychological and emotional aspects of her healing process, but as for her facing the charges against her, I am truly sorry that she will have to go through that. So, speaking now as a friend to your family, I would suggest that you all make up your minds to be an extension of her strength and support her as much as humanly possible. Evelyn has a strong spirit, and I'm far from religious, but if you ask me, all things considered I think she's got an angel watching over her and she's going to be just fine. So how about we all just agree to be optimistic at this point in time and see what happens."

Dr. Cole closed the folder containing Evelyn's chart and stood and shook Daniel's hand. He kindly nodded to Sabreena and

Marie before exiting and left the family to absorb their current situation. Sabreena, still visibly upset began fussing again, "And here I am being sucked into believing that there may actually be a ray of hope for us. Well so much for that idea. Excuse me for saying so mommy, but your God is cruel and relentless when it comes to us! And you know what else, the only reason why He let Evelyn live is to finish what He started, and that's torturing this family until the day that the very last one of us takes our last breath! If the two of you can't see that then you're both fools. I won't sit in that room with Eve singing "we shall overcome" and waiting on something miraculous to free her from her cuffs. The two of you can have it, I'm done!" Sabreena ranted as she grabbed her things. "I can catch a cab home. I'm outta here!" She continued angrily as she left the conference room.

Daniel sat quietly with his head in his hands covering his face, never making an attempt to stop his baby sister. He was emotionally exhausted and thought it best to just let Sabreena leave. Marie sat with her hands folded on top of her purse, and just shook her head in disappointment. The room was silent for a while. It was what they both needed at that moment. Marie could no longer keep her thoughts to herself, and she broke the silence, "Is she always this angry D? I tried really hard to make her get help before I left, and when that didn't work, I thought I could help. I realized one day that I had no idea how to get my little girl back. My brother took more than her innocence away from her that day; he raped her of her soul D. Now how can I ever restore those things?"

Marie vented on without realizing that Daniel had begun to cry. Then it dawned on her that Daniel always felt responsible for letting that happen. She hugged him and began to apologize, "I'm sorry baby, but you have to stop beating yourself up about that night. That sick bastard got the jump on you. He knew you were there, but you were unaware that he was there and was up to something so horrific. You two were only kids and there was no way y'all could have stood up to a man his size baby."

Marie grabbed Daniel's hand as she continued, "I wish I could turn back the hands of time and just change what happened that day, but I can't. I made the decision to go see an apartment with Eve. You went to the playground to play ball with your friends, and Bree stayed home alone for a while, which was nothing out of the ordinary. For years, we all have felt responsible in some kind of way for what happened to Bree. Forgiving myself, and placing the blame where it belonged, with my brother, was one of the hardest accomplishments for me when I was in therapy. But the truth is that your Uncle Byron is the only monster in this story, and baby, the rest of us are just as much as victims as Sabreena."

Marie pulled Daniel into her arms before she went on, "Now I am guilty of something, and I will spend the rest of my life, long or short, making it up to all of you. I'm guilty of giving up. D, I knew you were stealing liquor and drinking at the age of 13. I told myself that it was the only way you could sleep at night after living through what happened. I also knew that Bree was only 12 years old and couldn't wrap her mind around something so detestable happening to her, and at the hands of her own kin. But I was her mother, and it was my responsibility to make her get help. It was my responsibility to get all of us help. I was the only parent y'all had. Your father couldn't help himself to anything but a bottle, let alone help any of us. But I failed when it mattered most.

One day I woke up and two years had gone by, and we were a mess. Your father was dead; you were a lost child, trying desperately to drown your sorrows away with alcohol; Bree was an angry, scorned little girl who pretended that she was ok, and Eve, was the only thing holding the broken pieces together; but shame on me for putting that on her. She was 22 years young, and her life was just beginning. She was engaged to Troy, and she was ready to move out on her own when Bree was raped. She put her life on hold for two years and juggled between caring for us and trying to start a life with Troy.

Part of me believes that I was afraid that we would fall apart completely after Eve left home. I was afraid of things getting worse in her absence, so I left to get help. I thought that I would be able to help my children if I could just get myself together. As time went on and I saw that Eve managed to marry, get you two through school and out on your own, all while maintaining her own life; I started feeling like I was never going to be able measure up to her. Instead of even attempting to make things right with you and Bree, I made excuses as to why I shouldn't. I have regretted those choices ever since."

Marie, now looking like she was on the verge of tears continued, "I missed you and Bree's graduations, Eve's wedding, and only God knows what else. I can never get those things back. I let fear get in the way of me being the mother that I should have been for my children. I began to feel like I was so far removed from y'all, that only a miracle from God would reconnect us. I prayed all of the time for God to give me a chance at redemption in this lifetime. I never lost hope, and now that this chance has been given to me, I will fight until I draw my last breath to restore the relationships that we once had."

Daniel was now rubbing Marie's back in an attempt to comfort her as she poured out her heart to him. He looked at his mother with eyes full of compassion and said, "Mom, I forgive you. And now you have to stop beating yourself up about the past. We all made some poor decisions, and those usually lead to worse ones, but we can't change them, we can only learn from them and move forward. And to answer your question about Sabreena: Yes! She's always that angry, which is why I'm sure that I can remain sober. Because believe you me, the only thing I want to do after a day with my little sis, is have a drink!" Daniel said jokingly as he stood up and towered over his mother. He extended his hand to assist Marie in getting up from her chair. Then he proceeds, "Now let's get in here and see what's going on with our little jail bird before visiting hours are over. I hope she wakes up soon. I've been waiting for three months to see those brown eyes staring back at me."

Marie and Daniel walked arm in arm to Evelyn's room, mocking and joking about Sabreena's eventful exit. For the first time in years, they were giddy and laughing like old times. When they reached Evelyn's hospital room there was a nurse assisting Dr. Cole at Evelyn's side, so Marie and Daniel stood impatiently at the doorway waiting for them to finish. The nurse exited and shortly after, Dr. Cole followed. As the Dr. was leaving the room he smiled at Daniel and Marie and said, "She's all yours."

The two of them approached Evelyn anxiously. Daniel called out her name as Marie stood over her and rubbed her arm. Daniel began to talk to her as he did when

she was in the coma, "Hey sissy, it's D. I
don't know if you can hear me, but I'm here
visiting for a bit. Mommy's here too, but
Bree left after blowing up about your "state
issued bracelet". Please wake up sissy. I
just wanted to see those pretty browns
before we have to leave. Plus, Bree really
stressed me out and I could use some
cheering up before I go back home. And",
but he stopped abruptly, as he could see a
smile coming across Evelyn's face. She
couldn't hold it in any longer and she
cracked a full smile and uttered what
sounded like an angel singing to Daniel and
Marie, "Awe stop ya whining and gimme a
hug punk!" Evelyn said weakly, while
grinning from ear to ear.

She opened her eyes to a shocked,
but elated Daniel. He jumped back and
placed both hands on top of his head in
disbelief. It was what he needed in order to
really know that his sister was really alive.
He paced back and forth for a few seconds
while silent tears of joy dripped down his
face. Marie, already hugging Evelyn,
laughed and held her daughter tight as she
whispered praises of gratefulness into the
atmosphere.

Daniel finally took in fully, the sight of his sister alive, awake, and surprisingly lighthearted; and he nearly leaped into the hospital bed, knocking Marie sideways. Daniel wrapped his arms around Evelyn and spewed out, "Oh thank God for your stubbornness Sissy! I've missed you so much. I just can't believe you're awake." Daniel was squeezing so hard that Evelyn began to squirm. She yelped, "Yeesh, D! Loosen up a little before you squeeze me back into a coma." Daniel loosened his grip and backed away again to take in the sight of his big sister. With tears in his eyes, he shook his head and said, "Eve, you have no idea how I missed the sound of your voice nagging and fussing at me. Go ahead, yell some more. I cut your screen at your house, I threatened to slap baby sis...what else? I can't think of anything else right now but please, come on; yell!" Daniel babbled on hysterically until Evelyn cut him off saying, "boy shut-up and get back over here and hug me like you got good sense."

Daniel and Marie laughed through tears of joy. It was as if Evelyn had never lost consciousness. Mentally, she appeared to be her same old motherly, witty, snappy self again. With only an hour left for visiting, the three of them spent that little time trying to catch Evelyn up as much as possible. As their visit came to an end, they all wore heavy eyes feeling as if the next 12 hours or so would never pass. Marie and Daniel promised Evelyn that they would be back first thing the next morning, and with that they said their goodbyes and left Evelyn for the night.

Psalm 30:5

***...weeping may endure for a night,
but joy cometh in the morning.***

Sabreena didn't recognize the
number lighting up the screen on her cell
phone, so she declined to answer. After a
short pause, the number glowed across the
screen again. Highly irritated, Sabreena
snatched up the phone from her nightstand
and answered in a hiss, "who the heck is
this, and why are you calling me back-to-
back! You don't know how to leave a
message?"

The voice on the other end totally
caught Sabreena off guard when it
responded. "I see some things didn't change
much over the last three months." Evelyn
said in her all too familiar sassy tone.
"Sissy! Is this really you! I mean you
sound... You're... I can't believe... Wha?"
Sabreena fumbled trying to form a sentence.
Evelyn cut her short and snapped back,
"Humm, I take that back. Maybe some
things have changed, 'cuz I can't remember
a time in your life when you couldn't figure
out what to say out of that mouth of yours!"

Sabreena giggled and lightened up
immediately. "Hey Sissy, I'm sorry. I

wasn't expecting you on the other end when I picked up. I missed you so much. I still can't believe this is you. I ain't even gon' lie Sissy, I thought it was curtains for you. I'm sorry I left yesterday, but I was 'bouta tear some stuff up in that hospital when I saw them handcuffs on you. Shoot, you know I don't play that." Sabreena said sternly. "Did they take 'em off?" Sabreena asked.

Evelyn sighed before responding, "No Baby Sis, but you have to understand that they are just following protocol and doing their jobs." Then in a playful tone, Evelyn said jokingly, "besides, I am like the black widow up in this piece." But Sabreena couldn't find the humor in the situation, and she argued back saying, "Sissy, I'm serious! How can you joke about something like this! It killed me to see you lying up in that hospital like that, so I know I can't deal with visiting you in jail. Aren't you the least bit worried?"

Evelyn replied, "Baby girl, I know this may be hard to accept, but you're just gonna' have to trust me on this one. I will be fine, so stop worrying and get your butt down to this hospital so I can personally get on you about how you've been acting a fool

these last three months. Umm hmm, I heard
about it, and now you gon' hear my mouth,
'cuz I raised you better. Now get your little
funky attitude havin', split tail down here
before I pull a Kunta Kente and break outta
these cuffs to come after you."

Sabreena grunted, "Uggh, just when
I thought I was happy to hear your voice
again. Aight, I'm getting dressed now sissy.
Be there soon. But those cops betta respect
my gangsta'! I'm not one to be played with,
so they better recognize!" Sabreena and
Evelyn busted out laughing as Evelyn
retorted, "Whateva girl! Hurry up and get
down here. I miss your crazy self. Love
you little sis, see you when you get here.
And you better behave, 'cuz I'M the one not
to be played with. Bye."

They both shook their heads as they
hung up their phones, still laughing and
happily anticipating their reunion. Evelyn
looked up and noticed that she had an
unfamiliar visitor waiting. "Hello, can I
help you with something?" Evelyn asked as
she took in the sight of the tall, dark, slender
and handsome young man that stood in her
doorway. He immediately approached and
extended his hand as he replied, "Yes, my
name is Aaron. Your mother and I attend

the same church, and she has retained me as your lawyer. I have been informed that the detective handling your case will be here to get a statement from you around noon. I just wanted to speak with you before that happened to advise you on how to proceed with that. I also need your permission to get a written statement from your doctor about injuries in your past medical history, as well as the physical condition you were in when you arrived here three months ago."

Evelyn looked him up and down once more and replied. "Honey, are you even old enough to be someone's lawyer? You look like you're fresh out of high school." Aaron smiled and Evelyn was further impressed at the sight of his perfectly straight, pearly white teeth. He then answered, "Yes ma'am. I would be happy to supply you with my credentials, and my record in court speaks for itself. I aim to please and I'm certain that I won't disappoint. Furthermore, for what it's worth, I don't take on cases that I don't feel strongly about winning; not even for a sweet little lady like your mother, God bless her."

Evelyn smiled at the young man then she replied, "Well, you don't lack manners or confidence, and from what I can tell so far you seem to be brutally honest. So, I guess there's nothing left to this introduction." Then Evelyn leaned forward with one eyebrow turned up and snarled, "Except, don't call me ma'am. I'm not that old. Call me Eve; and it's my pleasure to have you represent me Aaron"

With the formalities out of the way, the two of them got down to the business of laying down the foundation of what would be the fight for the rest of Evelyn's life. Aaron was very thorough, and he left no stone unturned. He grilled and prepped Evelyn and she became more impressed with his skills as her lawyer as he asked questions that Evelyn would have never deemed important to her case.

They were so involved in this process that neither of them noticed Sabreena enter the room after a while. Sabreena cleared her throat to get their attention. She blew past Aaron and hugged her sister so tight; then she planted a juicy kiss on her forehead. "Ewe Bree, did you have to slime me?" Evelyn exclaimed. "Awe, don't act like you don't miss my kisses Sissy. I'm just so happy to see you like this; up and fussing, like usual." Sabreena said as they both laughed.

Sabreena then turned to Aaron and in an apologetic tone says, "I'm sorry, I have just been waiting for quite some time to see my sister this way again. I don't believe we've met. My name is Sabreena, I'm Evelyn's younger sister, much younger; and you are?" Sabreena extended her hand as she waited for Aaron's reply. Evelyn cocked her head back and smirked as she realized Sabreena's deliberate attempt to speak properly and show her manners.

Aaron replied as he stood up from his seat and shook Sabreena's hand, "My name is Aaron, and I will be representing Eve in her case. I am a fellow worshipper at the church that your mother attends. I have heard quite a bit about you from your mother, but it's nice to finally put a face to the name and all of the stories." He and Evelyn quickly noticed the change of expression on Sabreena's face after Aaron's reply. Evelyn grinned even harder, as she knew her baby sister all too well. As Sabreena pulled her hand away and crossed her arms, Evelyn mumbled under her breath, "Aaand here it comes, in 5,4,3."

But before Evelyn could even finish counting down, Sabreena blurted out, "Oh really, so what kind of foolish stories has mommy dearest been filling your head with church boy!" Evelyn, now embarrassed, covered her face with her free hand and peeked out between her fingers to see Aaron's reaction. Much to her surprise, He never even flinched or batted an eyelash. He grinned as he sat back down in his chair and crossed his legs then he looked up at Sabreena and smiled as he replied so charmingly, "I'll tell you what, we can discuss that further over dinner tomorrow night."

Sabreena, still baring her defensive pose, snapped back, "And what makes you think that I would ever have dinner with your kind!?" Aaron sat forward in his seat, still grinning, and he asked, "By my kind, do you mean a man or a Christian?" Evelyn now grinning from ear to ear at the sight of her sister meeting her wit's match; stared in anticipation to see her sister's response.

Sabreena, now feeling extremely challenged, unfolded her arms and leaned down into Aaron's personal space and answered through clinched teeth, "BOTH!" But Aaron remained unfazed, and he smirked at the sight of seeing Sabreena ruffled, he calmly responded, "Yeah, that's what I thought. And to answer your question; I know you'll have dinner with me because I know your kind. And before you ask, by your kind, I mean woman-angry; both! But it's ok, because I'm very well equipped to handle "your kind". Question is, little lady, can you handle "my kind" and by my kind I mean assertive, intelligent, well mannered, patient, successful, male, and yes Christian."

Aaron stood up and towered over Sabreena as he reached into his inside pocket to retrieve one of his business cards. Sabreena, now wearing a puzzled look, opened her mouth to speak but Aaron quickly raised his index finger and shook his head, no. He extended his card to her and said sternly, "And did I mention good looking? No need to respond, we can discuss that over dinner tomorrow as well. Here's my card, you can text the cell number with your address, and I will see you tomorrow around seven."

Sabreena snatched the card from his hand and stuffed it into her purse. Still wearing a look of confusion, she turned to Evelyn and said, "I don't have time for this craziness, I'm going down to the cafeteria until the two of you finish your business! You know how to reach me. Call me when it's "safe" to come back up!" Sabreena slid past Aaron, rolling her eyes at him as she passed, and she exited without saying goodbye to him.

When Evelyn felt that the coast was clear she shrieked with laughter. She slapped her leg as she gave Aaron his props, "Well done, if I must say so myself. I have to admit that was a first. I think I'm gonna like you Aaron, and you know what; I think my mother was up to something when she picked you for my lawyer. Umm hmm, and I'm not talking about just winning my case either. No sir. I see that Marie still got a few tricks left up her sleeve, and she knows her children better than I thought she did. Man, I wish my brother was here to see that one."

Evelyn was in awe at the way Aaron handled Sabreena. Aaron, still calm and unmoved by the exchange with Sabreena responded, "Well, I wouldn't be as good as I am, at what I do, if I let what people say get under my skin. Besides, Mrs. Williams gave me fair warning. So, in all honesty, I kind of had the upper hand going into that one; but let's just keep that our little secret." They both chuckled in agreement and then Evelyn asked, "So, are you staying with me while I give my statement? The detective will be here soon, it's almost noon." Aaron responded with his charming smile, "Yes ma'am... I, I mean Eve. I will be present during their questioning. And speak of the devil, here comes the detective now."

Aaron stood up to introduce himself to the detective. Evelyn went through the formality of introducing herself as well. The detective was anxious to get what he needed and go, so they wasted no time getting started. Evelyn took her time as she gave him a detailed report on the painstaking events that took place on that horrible morning. When she was done, the detective explained the process moving forward and then he left Evelyn with her lawyer.

When Aaron was sure that Evelyn was ok and understood clearly what was ahead of them, he left his contact information with Evelyn and ended his visit. As Evelyn sat alone in her hospital bed and relived in her mind, what she had just reported to her lawyer and the detective, a great sadness came over her. She loved Troy deeply and she missed the good times that marked the beginning of her and Troy's relationship. Though they were short lived, they were what Evelyn held on to over the years, and deep down inside, she hoped that they would one day find their way back to those times. But it would never be now, and that left a void in her.

Evelyn whose near-death experience had changed her in a very spiritual way, began to meditate to bring herself comfort. Breaking her silence, she began to speak quietly to her higher power:

Spirit,

In the last three months, I have connected with you from a place that no one could ever believe, yet alone imagine. You have shown me grace beyond what most can fathom, you have allowed me to rest until I was tired no more, you have forgiven me for the life that I have taken, you have given me the promise of peace, and blessed assurance, and you have granted me another chance at redemption. In my time of rest and unconsciousness, I found your secret place. I bask in the glory of now knowing that You and I are one. As I embark on the journey that is set before me, I will diligently reflect inward and ask that you give me the wisdom, knowledge, and understanding to do what is best. But most of all, I will continue to connect and consult with you through prayer and

*meditation for the strength and guidance to
weather the storm ahead of me.*

Ase'

Evelyn opened her eyes and reached
for her phone to call Sabreena. She then
noticed that she had a missed call from her
mother, so she decided to return her call
first. She was wondering where they were
since they promised to show up early that
morning. It was now well after noon, and
she wondered what happened as the phone
rang in her ear. Marie answered on the other
end, "Good afternoon sunshine. I know you
were looking for us this morning, but I had
Daniel take me over to Aaron's office to
retain him for you. I had a message from
the detective last night, saying he was
coming by the hospital to speak with you. I
was grateful for the heads up, and I know
Aaron is going to do a great job. D and I
decided to go have breakfast so that we
wouldn't be in the way when Aaron and the
detective came. So how did everything go?"
Marie finally asked.

Evelyn answered in a very perky
voice, "It went well. But I can't wait until
you and D get here so I can tell you the best
part. He checked Sabreena so hard that MY
ego was hurt. Yeah, not really, but it took

everything in me to maintain my composure and not crack up in her face. I think you knew exactly what you were doing by sending him. Didn't you mommy?" Marie laughed on the other end and responded coyly, "Why, I have no idea what you mean sweetie. Aaron's a good lawyer and I was thinking only of you my dear."

But Evelyn wasn't hearing it, she knew better, and she rebutted, "Yeah right mommy. All of those older and experienced lawyers in your church, and you send that tall dark cup of chocolate milk over here to my rescue, knowing darn well that Bree would cross his tracks eventually. Umm Hmm, you ain't slick lady. I know what you're up to. You're tryna kill two birds with one stone, and you figured he's exactly what she needs to cure her obscured ideas of being gay and her endless mission of rebuking the church. Now tell the truth and shame the devil woman."

Marie laughed so hard she had tears rolling down her face. "Alright, alright, you got me." Marie confessed as they both cracked up at the thought of Sabreena meeting her match. Marie continued saying, "I figured, he's tall, dark, handsome, and he argues for a living. Now how can she get around all of that? I would have loved to see him in action with her today. Guess I have to pray to see it next time. We are so bad for this, but Lord knows that child needed an intervention. She's awful!" And the two of them laughed even harder.

Evelyn caught her breath after laughing so hard and then asked, "So, are the two of you on your way?" Marie confirmed that they would be there shortly, and they ended their conversation. Evelyn then called Sabreena and let her know that all was clear and that she could come up to visit with her. As she waited for Sabreena to come up, she thought of the irony of her awful situation bringing her family back together. A broad smile spread across her face as a gentle warmth came over her. She closed her eyes and silently mouthed the words, "Thank you"! For the first time in years, she really believed that her family would be just fine.

Matthew 5:43-45

"You have heard that it was said, 'Love your neighbor and hate your enemy.' But I tell you, love your enemies and pray for those who persecute you, that you may be children of your Father in heaven. He causes his sun to rise on the evil and the good, and sends rain on the righteous and the unrighteous.

"I cannot believe that my little sister, the bully, is allowing herself to be bullied into a date; and with a Christian man at that. Baby sis, are you sure you're feeling okay?" Daniel teased at Sabreena as he accompanied her through the mall. "Oh, would you just give it a rest D! It's just dinner. And a girl's gotta eat right?" Sabreena challenged back at D. "Now shut your trap and help me find something to wear for tonight!" Sabreena spat as she crossed the threshold into the store. Daniel dropped his head and mumbled under his breath, "Eve has got to get well and win her freedom, cuz' I am not about to be shopping for clothes, in the mall, with my baby sister, every time she has a meet and eat".

Daniel trailed behind Sabreena clueless and now visibly annoyed at his current situation. "Oh, come on Bree, pick something already so we can get out of here! How the heck did I end up here with you anyway? You told me that you had to make a quick stop Bree! The post office is a quick stop. This? This is pure torture for a man" Daniel whined. "Awe quit crying. I'm almost done. Just let me try this stuff on and then I'm done. Besides, it ain't like you have anything better to do anyway" Sabreena fussed back at Daniel. "There's a seat. Sit down and relax for a sec. I'll be out in a sec so you can tell me what you think" Sabreena said as she went into the dressing room.

Daniel noticed the look of excitement on his little sister's face and decided to let her have this one. After all, it wasn't often that Sabreena showed signs of being anything but bitter. After a few minutes Sabreena came out of the dressing room wearing a form fitted dress that stopped just below her knees. Daniel's face balled up with intensity as he came to the realization that his sister wasn't a little girl anymore. "I don't like it. They don't have anything less... revealing? I'll go look. What size are you? Maybe I can find some nice dress pants and a pretty blouse. I'll look around while you take that off" Daniel babbled on, clearly perturbed at the sight of Sabreena in that dress.

"No need, this dress will do. Your reaction said it all" Sabreena said as she cracked up while turning back into the dressing room. "Bree, I'm serious. You are not wearing that dress anywhere! I'm putting my foot down. Now you put that thing back on the rack and try again" Daniel said sternly. "Yeah, yeah, yeah", Sabreena said as she came back out of the dressing room. Unfazed by Daniel's barking, Sabreena made her way to the register with Daniel, once again, trailing behind her, now even more annoyed than when they entered the store. "Fine! You can wear the dress, but I'm coming with you. Christian or no Christian, he's still a man", Daniel exclaimed.

Sabreena continued to wear a devilish smirk and shook her head as she paid for her dress and left the store with her brother. "D, calm down; I'm not a child anymore. I am a young lady and I know how to carry myself like one", Sabreena said in an attempt to ease her brother's worries. Daniel, remaining agitated, gritted his teeth and continued making his way back to the car in silence. The two of them made the trip back to Sabreena's place in uncomfortable silence. As he pulled up in front of her door, he attempted to calm himself so that he could wish his sister well on her date.

He put the car in park and leaned over to hug Sabreena. "I'm sorry for trippin' on you back there. It's just that I haven't seen you in anything but jeans and Timbs, or baggy sweats and sneakers since you were a kid. I know you're a well-behaved young lady now, I just think it was easier for me when you were being chased by women. I'm still not happy about the dress, but I have to respect your "gangsta" now that you're all grown up", Daniel said playfully as he gave Sabreena a loving punch on the arm. "You try really hard to enjoy yourself tonight baby sis. And don't run him off too quickly. Give the brother a chance before he hits the chopping block. After all, only God knows if there will ever be another victim, I mean man, after him", Daniel teased.

"Thanks bro. I'll try to take it easy on him, but I can't promise you anything. Besides, I need to even the score. Can't have him thinking that he can shut me up any time he gets ready", Sabreena retorted as she was getting out of the car. As she turned to shut the door behind her, she continued, "I will call you as soon as I get back home tonight, provided that I'm not arrested for disturbing the peace or something crazy like that". Daniel declined to reply and just shook his head and rubbed his forehead, as he thought about the likelihood of that actually occurring. He watched Sabreena enter the house and then pulled off saying aloud, "God help that man, for he knows not what he got himself into".

Sabreena laid her dress out on her bed and picked out her accessories and shoes to complete her outfit. She was a little confused at the fact that she could not wipe the silly little grin off of her face that she had been trying to fight all day. She thought, "What the heck is my problem? I'm never this giddy". She put on her Beyonce CD as it complemented her mood as she prepared for her date. She danced around and sang along with B until she was showered, primped and pressed. She gave herself one last glance in the full-length mirror. Quite satisfied with what she saw reflecting back at her, she blew a kiss at herself and then uttered, "Umm hmm, I got something for Mr. Chocolate, Too Tall, Know it All".

Sabreena made her way downstairs to wait for Aaron to arrive. After about fifteen minutes she heard a knock at the door. She opened it to find Aaron standing there looking better and even more clean cut than she remembered. She invited him in while she grabbed her coat and her purse. Just like the gentleman he was, Aaron complimented her on how great she looked, helped her into her coat, and escorted her to his car. Sabreena, although she was too stubborn to admit, was more than impressed with Aaron so far.

As she sashayed down the front steps, she looked up to see what wheels Aaron was sporting. "Not bad Mr. big time lawyer; a 2021 Porsche Cayenne Turbo GT. So, the brother has expensive taste I see. I like, I like it a lot", Sabreena said playfully as she ducked into the vehicle with Aaron's assistance. Aaron, now impressed with Sabreena's knowledge of cars said, "It's so refreshing to accompany a lady who has good taste in men as well as an above average knowledge of cars". Of course, Sabreena being the tough act that she was could not let that comment about her taste in men slide by as she retorted, "well you're right about one thing, but we'll have to see about the other". And with that being said, the ice was broken and the two of them engaged in friendly conversation as they made their way to the restaurant.

Sabreena hated surprises, but she agreed in advance to let Aaron keep their plans under wraps, allowing her to be pleasantly surprised as their evening unfolded. When Aaron's car came to its final stop, Sabreena could not believe her eyes. She blurted out, "Oh, heck no! Is this Vetri, one of the most expensive Italian restaurants in Philly? Hold on a sec Mr. Too Tall, we need to lay down some ground rules. First and foremost, you are spending at your own risk tonight. Do not, and I repeat DO NOT expect anything in return but a thank you, a friendly hug and a strong compliment. Second of all-".

Aaron threw his hand up to hush Sabreena and interrupted, "little lady, get over yourself. Stop thinking so much and let's just enjoy the evening. I'm a hardcore Christian. Whether you believe it or not, I do not let my flesh get ahead of my love for God. So just an FYI for you, if we don't plan on catching a red eye to Vegas tonight, then I assure you that you have nothing, I repeat, NOTHING to worry about. Now can I give the valet the keys so we can get on with our date?" Sabreena, stifled once again, exited the vehicle, latched on to Aaron's arm, and entered the restaurant quietly.

Aaron, at his own suggestion and Sabreena's approval, ordered their meals as well as a fine bottle of wine for the two of them. The date was going well, and the conversation remained friendly and flowing. Aaron knew more about Sabreena than he initially admitted to. As the evening went on, he felt so sorry about what had happened to Sabreena many years ago. He couldn't help but see what a beautiful, intelligent, and caring young woman was hiding behind the course, hardened, helpless, bitter, and deeply hurt little girl. He wanted so much to help free her from that little girl, but he knew that it would be a fight far worse than any he's ever engaged in any courtroom. Before their date ended, Aaron had made the decision that she was worth the fight.

As the evening winded down and Aaron and Sabreena were on their way to her home, Aaron decided that it was time to let Sabreena know just how much he knew. He started a conversation treading softly, even though he already knew where it would end up, but it had to be done. "Sabreena, I need to tell you something, but before I do, I need you to promise me that you won't blow up" Aaron said softly. "What is it? And I can't promise you that. I've learned to express myself freely, and I won't refrain from doing that for anyone, but go on" Sabreena replied. Aaron continues, "Well first I want to say that I really enjoyed your company tonight, and I hope that you will consider going out with me again. I know this is our first date, but I feel like there's a strong chemistry between us, and I would love the chance to see where this is going. This is why I need to be honest with you about something before we go any further".

Sabreena interrupted, "Oh boy, here it comes. I knew it was too good to be true. So, what is it? You're married or some kind of mob lawyer who defends big time criminals? Come on out with it. Which one is it Mr. Too Tall?" Aaron couldn't help but laugh at Sabreena's outburst as he replied, "None of the above little lady. I need you to hear me out. I was one of your mother's counselors in the church's therapy program. She disclosed a lot of her personal information to me. That also led to her disclosing some things about you because it was affecting her ability to cope with life. Sabreena, I am really fond of you, and I want to help you press forward with your life. You're not going to like what I'm about to say, but your journey to healing begins with you forgiving."

Sabreena couldn't hold it in any longer, "How dare you! You have no idea what I feel inside, and you fix your mouth to

tell me to forgive? Pull over and let me out.
I will walk all the way home before I listen to
this mess! I mean it Aaron, pull over and let
me out now!" Sabreena demanded. Aaron
slowed down and pulled over and began to
plead, "Sabreena wait. Please just hear me
out. I'm not trying to pretend that I could
even imagine being in your shoes, but I know
what the scriptures say about forgiveness and
loving your enemies. I just think that you're
giving your uncle power over you as long as
you hold on to what happened. I saw a side
of you tonight that your family probably
never sees, and I want so much to help you be
that way all the time, but you have to trust
that what I'm saying is right."

Sabreena opened the car door and got
out of the car. She leaned in and said, "You
can take your scriptures, along with your
bright ideas and your know it all attitude, and
go straight to... to; I don't care where you go,
just stay the hell away from me! I don't need
saving. I was fine with my life before you
walked through that door yesterday, and I'm
going to be just fine after I walk away from
you tonight! Now you go on and have
yourself a "blessed night" Mr. Too Tall."
Sabreena made sure to slam his car door and
she walked away.

Aaron turned off his car, got out, and ran to catch up with Sabreena. "I won't let you walk alone, so I guess we'll both be taking this sixteen mile walk across town together. I'm fully aware of the fact that this is how you always successfully push people away. But check the record Sabreena, I'm a lawyer. Fighting and arguing is my job and I do it well. So, say what you will about me or to me, but you won't push me away that easy. And are we really going to walk all the way to your home? This is crazy Sabreena, come back to the car. We don't have to talk any more tonight; I just want to get you home safe. Now please come back to the car with me?"

Sabreena stopped in her tracks and turned to face Aaron. Through clinched teeth and a twisted-up face she spat back, "Fine, since you are begging!" and the two of them walked back to the car in complete silence. The ride to Sabreena's home seemed to take forever. Aaron walked Sabreena all the way to her door and stood unmoved as she entered and slammed the door in his face. Sabreena ran up to her room and balled up on her bed, fully clothed. As she began to cry silently, thoughts of her dreadful past filled her head. Before she even knew it, she had cried herself to sleep.

1 Corinthians 4:5

5 Therefore judge nothing before the time, until the Lord come, who both will bring to light the hidden things of darkness, and will make manifest the counsels of the hearts: and then shall every man have praise of God.

Sabreena woke up the next day to several missed calls and a splitting headache! She scrolled through her list of missed calls and huffed in disappointment. Only repeated attempts to reach her from Eve and D. She didn't understand why, but she had hoped that at least one of those missed calls would have been from Aaron. She checked her messages, tossed her phone on her bed, and headed towards her bathroom to draw herself a bath. "Screw everything and everyone!", Sabreena mumbled as she tossed the bath salts into the warm water.

"I'm gonna sit in my big tub, with my big attitude, and soak until all of the big pains in my butt don't matter anymore. Who needs a man anyway?" Sabreena said as slow tears rolled down her face. She slid down into the deep soaking tub and let the warmth and the smell of lavender take her mind away from her problems. After a long while, Sabreena was jolted from her serene soaking by the sound of her doorbell ringing repeatedly.

"What in the HELL!?", Sabreena snapped under her breath as she reached for her bath robe. She hurried down the hall and then down the steps, clearly pissed at the interruption. As she made her way to the door she began to yell in frustration. "Somebody better be dead, dying, or my house better be in danger of blowing up in the next thirty seconds! 'Cause I SWEAR stupidity will not be accepted as the reason why whomever you are, is ringing my damn bell like you're crazy!"

Sabreena flung the door open to find Daniel standing there looking frantic. "D! what the heck--"? But before Sabreena could finish her sentence, Daniel grabbed her and squeezed her tight. Sabreena, now totally confused and nervous at the thought of what drama could possibly be going on now, just stood there in Daniels arms, bracing herself for bad news. Daniel released her and the look on his face suddenly switched from frantic to furious. "Sabreena! I've been calling for hours! Why haven't you answered or returned my calls? I thought it was happening again!

Why would you not answer?!" Daniel
ranted.

In an instant, Sabreena's thoughts
reverted back to the night that Daniel found
Troy dead and Eve nearly dead, and she
understood why Daniel was so upset. "I'm
sorry D. I was bummed out about my date
last night. I didn't mean to scare you. I saw
the missed calls and I was gonna call you as
soon as I got out of the tub. I just wasn't
ready to talk to anyone yet. I wasn't
thinking. I should've let everyone know I
got home safe last night, but I must've cried
myself to sleep. And don't ask! Please...
Still not ready to talk about it!" Sabreena
exclaimed.

Daniel closed the door as he made
his way into the foyer. They both made
their way to the kitchen. Sabreena put on
coffee as Daniel made himself comfortable.
"So, Mr. Too Tall was a flop? We were all
banking on him taming our little fire
breathing dragon", Daniel teased. "D that's
not funny! I'm not that bad, am I?", asked
Sabreena. "I wonder who won that game
last night"., Daniel said as he looked up at
the ceiling... clearly evading Sabreena's
question. "Touché!", Sabreena huffed under
her breath as she pulled some fresh fruit out

of her fridge. Sabreena sat down in
complete silence for a minute. Daniel could
tell that she was in deep thought. "Go ahead
Bree. Ask away", Daniel said reluctantly.

Sabreena had been replaying last
night's events in her head over and over.
She felt needed an honest opinion from a
man. An opinion that she valued and
trusted, so she opted to seek advice from her
older brother. "D, do you think my choice
to date women came from an honest place?
I'm asking because it bothers me to think
that I went that route bogusly, when people
really struggle to be comfortable with their
sexuality. I never meant to hurt Inez or
make light of her lifestyle.", Bree asked.
Daniel thought for a moment before replying
sincerely, "Bree, I never really thought
about it. But now that you've asked, I feel
like it was a response to your trauma. Inez
knows you well enough to know that there
was no malice behind your choice. We all
know how difficult it must be to find some
sense of normalcy after what happened. I
could barely make it through breakfast
before having a drink. I knew for quite some
time that my drinking was well beyond out
of control, but I didn't want to remember
that night. I think that if you were strong
enough to never pick up a substance to cope

with what happened to you, then your being confused about your sexuality was just a harmless way for you to cope".

Sabreena was pleased with her brother's answer, but that wasn't the only storm brewing in that head of hers. She hesitated before asking Daniel, "Do you think I should give Aaron a chance"? Daniel replied, "I don't even know what happened last night, so I can't give you an honest answer". Sabreena began to explain, "He knew about my past. He was one of the people from mommy's church program that helped her through her grief. He told me I needed to forgive, basically for my own sake. He seems to think that it's making me bitter instead of better. But I"—Daniel interrupted, "He's right Bree. You've been angry for so long that it eats away at the sweet parts of you at times. Don't let our uncle get away with stealing your innocence and your soul. That man died a horrible death in jail. I feel like that was your justice. I think it's time to forgive yourself for feeling powerless. Try your best to let someone help you heal so that your life is not defined by what he did. Take your power back from him. You're stronger than his weak and sick ass transgressions against you".

Surprisingly, Bree was taking it all in without feeling like she wanted to explode, which was her normal response. Daniel noticed how surprisingly calm she was, and he asked, "You're fond of him, aren't you"? Oh snap! Baby sis caught some feelings for Mr. Too Tall"! Let me find out Marie picked up some match making skills on her journey. Well, I'll be damned"! Daniel took full advantage of this moment of vulnerability being displayed by Sabreena. Daniel continued playfully, "I think my work is done here. I'll be on my way so you can call your little boyfriend to kiss and make-up". "SHUT UP D", Sabreena screeched as she punched her brother playfully in the arm. But you could clearly see by the grin on her face that she was warming up to the thought of seeing where things would go with her and Aaron. Sabreena hugged her brother on his way out of the door. She grabbed her phone and shot Aaron a quick text that read: *"I'm sorry for the way our date ended. I enjoyed myself overall. I just get emotional about my past. Do you think we can try again"?* After what felt like minutes, but was really a few seconds that passed, Aaron replied, *"I'll pick you up on Saturday at noon. Wear something comfortable and suitable for outdoors. Ttyl".*

Galatians 5:16-17

"I say then: Walk in the Spirit, and you shall not fulfill the lust of the flesh. For the flesh lusts against the Spirit, and the Spirit against the flesh; and these are contrary to one another, so that you do not do the things that you wish." Galatians 5:16-17

Daniel decided to continue on with his day after laying eyes on Sabreena. But for the first time in months, he felt something that he hadn't been feeling- he was so on edge that he muttered, "I need a damn drink"! He stopped in his tracks with feelings of fear and confusion as the words slipped from his own mouth.   The mere thought of what he'd just said made him feel guilty, as if he'd already succumb to the urge. He felt short winded and sat down on some nearby steps. Daniel was overwhelmed with emotions. He placed his head in his hands and began to sob uncontrollably. He was aware that he was in public and struggled to pull himself together, enough to stop the sounds of his emotional distress from coming through, but the tears kept right on rolling down his cheeks.

Daniel felt a gentle tap on his shoulder. He looked up through his teary eyes to see a gentleman standing with a handkerchief extended. "As-salamu alaykum my good brother. You wanna come inside and talk about it", the stranger asked. Daniel looked in the direction in which the man was pointing. He didn't realize that he was sitting on the steps of a local Masjid. "Oh—I'm uhh... I wasn't... I apologize sir", Daniel replied. "No need to apologize. My name is Hassan. I'm the Imam here. Come in and talk for a minute. No pressure, just offering an ear", the stranger responded. Daniel, still in an emotional haze, decided to take the man up on his offer and go inside.

He began to express why he came to tears on the steps. Then something came over him and he started pouring his heart out to the Imam about everything that had happened in his life that led him to his active struggle with alcohol addiction and his bouts of depression. Daniel and Hassan talked for over two hours before the Imam invited Daniel to come back after prayer. Daniel realized how relieved he felt, being able to unload for the first time in forever. He agreed to return to the Masjid later to speak to Hassan, not just about his problems, but about Islam as well.

Daniel whispered to himself, "what are the odds of me having a moment of weakness at that very time at that very location? It HAS to be a sign!". Daniel went to the local deli to grab something to eat, but all he could think about was getting back to the Masjid to continue speaking with Hassan. He hadn't felt this good in years! He ate his sandwich while slow walking back to the Masjid, but he remained in deep thought. As he approached the steps of the building, he said under his breath, "I'm doing this… I'm going to take my shahada. I don't believe that today was a coincidence. It saved my life!".

Hassan was pleased to hear the news once Daniel entered the Masjid and informed the Imam of his sudden decision. In that moment, Daniel didn't know much about Islam, except that they prayed five times a day. He told himself that if he was given the responsibility to stop everything and connect with God five times a day, he had a better chance of never wandering off into someone's pub. It was an unorthodox way of embracing the religion, but it made all the sense in the world to him. The other

Muslims made him feel welcomed
immediately and somehow Daniel knew,
this path to stay connected to something
greater than him was exactly what his life
needed.

He left the Masjid that Evening with
a feeling of confidence and renewal. He
didn't feel like he would have to carry the
burdens of a man on his back all alone. He
knew he was expected to be the rock and the
protector for his mother and his sisters.
Only now, it didn't feel like he'd have to go
it alone, misunderstood and under
supported. He knew that he'd have the
understanding and support of his Muslim
community, and that made the thought of it
all a much easier one to bare. Daniel pulled
out his cell phone and tapped on Evelyn's
number. "Hey Bro! What you up to?",
Evelyn said cheerfully as she answered the
call. "Eve, you will never guess how my
day went. I want to tell you in person. I'm
on my way to visit you now. See you in a
few sis!". Daniel hung up and made a B-
line to Evelyn to share his news.

2 Peter 1:20-21

"20 Above all, you know this: No prophecy of Scripture comes from the prophet's own interpretation, 21 because no prophecy ever came by the will of man; instead, men spoke from God as they were carried along by the Holy Spirit."

Evelyn sat, staring out of the window with her head tilted to the sun. She imagined herself laying in a field of grass with the feeling of the sun's warmth dancing on her melanated skin. She reflected back to a time when things were good between her and Troy. A time when they did not have much but each other. Her memory traveled to the time that he prepared a picnic for her out by the local lake. He blindfolded her for the entire car ride. He made her stand blindfolded in the grass as he set the blanket out on the grass and prepared their lunch, lakeside. The sun's warmth danced around on her skin as she moved her head up and down, trying to peek through the top and bottom of the blindfold. A single tear ran down her face as she thought of the soft gentle kiss Troy had placed on her neck before he untied the blindfold. Evelyn was becoming overly emotional as she remembered how much in love they were back then. Suddenly her thoughts propelled forward to the tragic night that led her to take Troy's life and landed her in a coma. Her eyes began to well up with tears, and just as she felt she wanted to sob; Daniel entered the room and broke her train of thought. "Eve, I don't know how you'll feel about this, but I did something lifechanging for me today", Daniel blurted out before he was even fully in her sight. Evelyn quickly wiped her eyes and put a wide smile on her face before turning to greet her brother. "Well come on D—spit it out already! You know you hold news about as well as a food strainer holds water", Evelyn said playfully to hide her own sorrowful mood.

Daniel was excited as he went over today's events with his sister. Evelyn saw the extent of her brother's joy in his eyes as he spoke, but most importantly, she could feel the sincerity and the sense of relief that his energy emitted. She understood that her brother bared a lot of burden for the past. She knew how important it was for him to never drop the ball again when it came to being there for his sisters. She listened with joy in her own heart, for she too worried about the weight of the burdens pushing her brother back to a bottle. "Well don't just sit here Eve. Say something!", Daniel spat, breaking Evelyn out of her thoughts. "This is good news D. Islam? I have to say that I wasn't expecting that, but I truly believe that the Most High individually designs our paths in a way that fits us personally. I'm so glad that you didn't take that drink. Not just for us, but I think it would have destroyed you the most. D, you have a gigantic heart. God knows that; so, it's no surprise to me that He would make sure you were right where you needed to be when you had that moment of weakness. Trust me D, if anyone knows how "on time" God is, it's me little brother", Evelyn said with a coy smirk.

Daniel took a step back and looked at his sister with confusion. "You alright sis?", Daniel asked. Evelyn, now confused at his question replied, "Yeah, why do you ask"? Daniel paced back and forth before responding with honesty, "I don't know sis. I guess over the years I started to believe that you didn't believe in God. I actually braced myself for some kind of intellectual and analytical speech about how this will be a phase and I'm just triggered and I'm responding out of fear or grief or yada yada yada" --- "BOY SHUT UP", Evelyn interrupted! Daniel froze mid stride and they both burst out laughing. Evelyn regained a serious composure before pointing to a chair in the room and requesting Daniel to sit and listen carefully.

Evelyn began to speak, "D, something happened to me that I can't really explain clearly. I think I may have died or something weird like that. I know you all say I was in a coma, but I have memories of being here. Only my life was different, and it still doesn't feel like it was a dream. It felt like I was in the future or maybe in another version of our lives. Everything was so good, and our lives seemed kind of perfect. Only I opened my eyes, and I was in cuffs and people were standing over me explaining that I've been in a hospital for weeks. I know this is going to sound crazy, but it's like I see things differently now. I feel things differently. I know everyone is worried about the outcome of my trial, but I heard something so clear, tell me that I was completely fine, and I have nothing to worry about. In fact, I feel like I'm being told that we all are in good hands and that our worse times are behind us".

Evelyn continued, "D, I even pray differently. I feel an electrified sensation come over me when I pray. Then I feel a deep calmness and I just sit in it, and I swear to you Bro, I can hear something whispering to me in the midst of my calm. It tells me that my prayers are being answered and there's nothing I need to do but be still and let God work. Crazy right? I know".

Daniel listened in awe, immediately wanting to experience what his sister was speaking of. He broke his silence saying, "Eve, I don't even know what to say. Except I believe all of it. I hope I get to feel that sense of peace and confidence that Allah is working wonders in my life. I know Islam is nothing like what our family traditionally practiced in the past, but I really feel like it's for me sis". Eve adorned the biggest smile before replying, "Well then go for it D. I love this for you! I pray your alignment with and service to Allah brings you the highest and greatest outcome of your life! God knows you deserve that little brother. I feel like we all do".

Daniel, extremely emotional, got up and gave Evelyn the biggest heartfelt hug. "Uggghhh! Get ya musty underarms outta here boy!" Evelyn said playfully while Daniel squeezed harder. Daniel held on longer and retorted, "Stop calling me boy! I'm a man. Smell the difference and gimme my respect"! They both laughed uncontrollably as Evelyn pushed her brother away. Daniel finished up his visit with Evelyn on a good note and left the hospital with a new outlook on life as well as a feeling of optimism about everything to come. Daniel stood outside of the hospital and looked up to the sky and mouthed the words, "Thank You", before being on his way. For the first time in forever, he felt that all was truly well within him.

1 Corinthians 13:4

"Love is patient, love is kind. It does not envy, it does not boast, it is not proud". – 1 Corinthians 13:4

Sabreena hopped out of the bed in a frenzy. "I can't believe I slept this late! It's 10 am. How the heck am I supposed to get myself together by noon?", Sabreena yelled into the speaker phone at Evelyn on the other end. Evelyn answered, tickled "I'm glad I called, Sleeping Beauty. We can't let you mess this up before my trial is over". "Shut Up Eve! This isn't funny. I'm nervous enough about the date. I don't need you making it worse", Sabreena spat back in a frustrated tone. "Oh, get over yourself sis! Just get cleaned up and keep the rest simple. I'm sure Aaron is gonna love the sight of you, no matter what you put on. God knows this date is all he's been talking about; but don't tell him I told you that", Eve replied.

Sabreena couldn't help but to grin from ear to ear at that revelation. "I'll call you later sissy. I need to get a move on. I love you sis", Sabreena yelled into the phone from across her bedroom. Evelyn said her goodbyes and ended the call. Sabreena bumped up her music and rummaged through her closet to find the perfect outfit for her date. "Yellow it is", Sabreena said proudly as she laid her sundress across her bed. She soaked in a nice warm bath as she let her mind wander about what secret plans Aaron had lined up for the two of them. She cut her soak short and made sure her skin and hair were on point, just in time for Aaron's arrival.

The bell rang at 12 noon on the dot. Sabreena took a deep breath to calm her nerves before opening the door and planting her eyes on the tall, sexy, chiseled man on her steps. Aaron paused briefly, apparently just as blown away at the sight of Sabreena standing there. "Madam Sabreena, you chariot awaits", Aaron said playfully as he extended his arm to escort Sabreena to the car. Aaron opened her door and gently guided her in before closing the door and allowing the widest smile to adorn his face before reaching the other side of the vehicle. "Breathtakingly beautiful", Aaron whispered under his breath before he got into the car. He took one more glance at Sabreena before pulling off, as if to make certain that she was really there with him, then off they went.

They drove for nearly an hour before reaching their destination. They were enjoying the breeze and the sounds of an

Ol'School R&B playlist coming through the speakers. Sabreena was so engulfed in the song on the radio that she didn't realize Aaron had parked. She looked out to see that they were cliffside, surrounded by nothing but beautiful landscapes and outlines of the cities below them. "Oh my God Aaron. Where are we? It's so beautiful up here", Sabreena asked while acknowledging the flooding of butterflies forming in her belly.

Aaron replied as he opened his trunk, "I used to live about a mile from here when I was a teen. I found this place one day while I was bike riding. It became my private little place where I would come to think or sort out my emotions. It's very special to me, so I wanted to share it with you". Sabreena was so busy taking in the sights that she didn't notice that Aaron sat out a blanket and an entire spread for them within minutes. "Come sit with me, beautiful", Aaron said smoothly while extending his hand out to Sabreena. She turned around and gasped with her hands planted on her cheeks she exclaimed, "Wow, this is so dope!". Aaron laughed at the rawness of her expression. "Are you planning on feeding me too?", Sabreena asked coyly. "Nope! I did all the work so far, so you can have a seat right here and feed me while we catch up and get to know each other a little better", Aaron replied confidently.

Sabreena surprisingly did not hesitate to join Aaron on the blanket. Aaron pulled a travel size pillow from the tuck and gently placed it on Sabreena's lap. He placed his head on the pillow, looking up at her and then folded his arms across his chest. "Grapes please', Aaron said playfully as he sat with his mouth open, waiting to be fed. Sabreena chuckled as she fed him single grapes and just like that, she was comfortable in his company. The day seemed to be going by quickly as the two of them conversed openly and took turns feeding each other. Before either of them knew it, the sun was setting, and their date would have to come to an end.

The music played in the background as they both sat quietly during the drive home. They were feeling bittersweet at the success of their date but both not wanting the day to come to an end. Aaron began to grow nervous as he pulled up to Sabreena's home. He wrestled with how much of a "goodbye" was within Sabreena's comfort zone. As he opened the door to let Sabreena out, she reached for his hand and allowed

herself to stand just close enough to invite
Aaron into her personal space. It was as if
she knew that he was struggling to read her
level of comfort with him.

Aaron pulled her in closer and held
her firmly. He gave her the sweetest
embrace while planting a soft kiss on her
bare shoulder, but not quite on the neck.
Sabreena thought she'd just melt on the spot,
but she mustered the strength to maintain
her composure. Aaron loosened his hold
and grabbed her by the hand as he led her to
her door. The emotions were so intense
between them in that moment that a deaf
person could hear their hearts beating
through their chests. Aaron turned to her
once more and planted a sweet kiss on her
forehead before guiding her into her door.
He watched as she turned to walk into her
home and stayed planted until her door shut
behind her.

Sabreena peeked through a window
as Aaron walked back to his car. He
glanced backwards before getting in, as if he
knew he was being watched. He sat in the
car for a minute, taking everything in before
pulling off. Sabreena continued watching
until the glare of his brake lights were out of
her line of sight. She then let out a long sigh

as if she hadn't taken a breath all day. "Oh my God, am I falling for this man?", she thought to herself. She dug down in her purse to retrieve her cell phone and immediately dialed Evelyn's number.

"Well...spit it out", Evelyn said as she answered excitedly. "Well damn. Hello Eve", Sabreena retorted. "Yeah, yeah, yeah, whatever! How'd it go? Where'd he take you? Did you enjoy yourself? Did you chase him away this time?", Evelyn ran off with questions. "EVE! Let me talk! Yeesh!", Sabreena exclaimed. "Let me patch D in so you don't have to tell us everything twice. Hold on a sec", Evelyn said as she dialed and linked Daniel in on the call.

"Ok, D is here. Now spill it", Evelyn said anxiously. Sabreena raced to her room and allowed herself to fall backwards freely onto her bed. She spared no details as she filled Eve and D in on the specifics of her beautiful day from start to finish. Evelyn and Daniel did not stop at the chance to tease playfully while Sabreena happily gloated. As they were in the midst of their celebratory conversation, Evelyn received a text message. She pulled the phone away from her ear to check it. It was from Aaron. Evelyn opened it to read: "*I have to wrap up this case with you asap. Between me and you, you will be my sister-in-law one day and I'm gonna make damn sure that you're free to give my bride away. Have a good night sis.*"

Evelyn rejoiced silently as she hearted the message, then happily reengaged in the conversation with her siblings. She wasn't certain about everything in life, but she was sure that if anyone deserved to have a happily ever after life, it was her little sister. "So, when's the next death match...I meant date, baby sis?", Evelyn teased as she chimed in. The three of them cracked up at the question, as they all knew how difficult Sabreena could be. "I don't know sis, but I hope it's soon. I don't believe I'm saying this but, I miss him already. I'm on a natural high and I don't wanna come down. I really like him y'all", Sabreena rattled off.

The moments of silence over the phone that followed was evidence of the state of shock that Sabreena's statements had put her siblings in. "Well don't everybody speak at once!", Sabreena blurted out, breaking the silence. They all laughed in unison before wrapping up the call and leaving Sabreena to bask in her blissful mood.

Sabreena closed her eyes and replayed the events of her day over and over. She adorned the widest smile as the nostalgic emotions overtook her senses. She could still smell his cologne on her clothes, and she felt as if she could still feel his fingers gently passing through her hair as she thought about laying on the blanket close to him, sharing intimate details of their lives. Sabreena's thoughts were interrupted by the sound of her phone notifying her of an incoming text.

Sabreena opened her eyes feeling a bit annoyed by the interruption but was soon overjoyed seeing that the message was from Aaron. She fumbled the phone while opening the text message. Her heart literally melted as she read its contents: ***"Things I already admire about you: Your laugh is an octave below a screech when you're slightly embarrassed. Your eyes are the perfect shade of teddy bear brown. Your hair has natural streaks of reddish-brown throughout it that sparks thoughts of an autumn sunset, and your curls are extra coiled at the tips. Your complexion is like a dark cup of coffee with a touch of cream.***

Your natural fragrance is like a fresh picked honey suckle flower. Last but not least; your smile is perfect and could illuminate the earth before The Creator spoke the command of light. You're the definition of beautiful, inside and out and your energy is unmatched. I'm honored that you're trusting me to exist in your energy. I hope you enjoyed our time together and I look forward to the next. Goodnight beautiful".

Heartfelt tears streamed down Sabreena's face and pooled onto her pillow as she silently cried tears of joy and battled her thoughts of disbelief. She never imagined that anything good could happen to her. She didn't want to think that Aaron was shaping up to be too good to be true, but it crossed her mind. She shook away the negative thoughts as fast as they entered her mind.

Sabreena was at a loss for words and felt that no exchange of words in response to Aaron's text would suffice. She "hearted" the message and hoped that Aaron wouldn't take it as a sign of unappreciation or disinterest. "Ok, cool shower then off to bed", Sabreena spoke out loud to herself. Sabreena let the thoughts reemerge as the water beat against her. She couldn't describe what she was feeling but she knew it was like nothing she'd ever felt before, and she loved it.

Sabreena finished her shower and settled into bed. She opened up her photos and began surfing through the pictures that she and Aaron had taken. She stopped and zoomed in on one particular photo. It was a selfie that caught Aaron in the short distance, with a look of pure admiration on his face. She grinned from ear to ear as she sent the photo to Aaron with the caption: "***The perfect photobomb. Goodnight***", and a single purple heart.

Sabreena thought that the discovery of the photo was the perfect ending to her night. She struggled with the thought that then crossed her mind, but then surrendered to it. "I feel like I should pray", She thought silently. This wasn't something that she was used to doing, so she decided to keep it short and sweet. She folded her hands across her chest and closed her eyes and spoke aloud. "God? I just want to say thank you. I want to believe that I deserve goodness in my life. Please let me be right. Amen". Sabreena allowed herself to drift off to sleep shortly after.

Isaiah 30:18

"And therefore will the Lord wait,
that he may be gracious unto you,
and therefore will he be exalted,
that he may have mercy upon you:
for the Lord is a God of judgment:
blessed are all they that wait for him"

Evelyn scurried around her bedroom looking for the perfect accessories to accentuate her outfit. It had been months since she had been discharged from that dreary hospital and completed her physical therapy. Aaron, being the skilled and reputable attorney that he was, was able to successfully get a judge to grant Evelyn monitored house arrest until her trial determined her fate.

Today was that day. Her trail was coming to an end, and she would soon learn the outcome of it all. She hated that damn ankle monitor but learned to be grateful for not having to deal with the alternative, a prison cell. "Eve! What are you doing up there?! I've made Salat and then breakfast and ate and you're STILL not ready", Daniel yelled from downstairs. "And what are you over there doing Bre?! With that dumb grin on your face...Ugghh! Never mind. I already know...you're texting Aaron.

Shouldn't he be focused on closing out this trial?", Daniel spat at Sabreena.

"D calm down. Take some deep breaths and have several seats. You're not helping and all that barking ain't gon' make her come down them stairs no sooner", Sabreena snapped back at Daniel while rolling and cutting her eyes. Daniel quickly accepted defeat, grabbed the remote control and plopped down into the couch while powering on the television. Ten minutes later, a nervous but well-dressed Evelyn came down and rushed her siblings out of the door.

They met Aaron outside of the courthouse and they all entered together. Sabreena and Daniel made their way to the seating gallery as Aaron and Evelyn went off to a conference room to discuss the closing arguments. It wasn't long before Evelyn's case was up and Aaron was before them, delivering his closing arguments, then off went the jury to deliberate.

One hour later, Evelyn found herself standing before a Judge, a jury and a room full of people waiting to hear what would happen to the woman who "allegedly" defended herself with deadly force against her abusive, alcoholic husband.

Nonetheless, Evelyn stood hand in hand with Aaron as the verdict was read. It was a good thing that they were standing so close because just as the words left the court clerk's mouth, Evelyn passed out in total disbelief.

Everything was happening so fast. Court personnel rushed to Evelyn's aid as they called for emergency help. Sabreena and Daniel were being held back and calmed by court officers. Sabreena's cries for her sister could be heard through multiple court rooms. Daniel had to pull himself together and help the only sister he could gain access to in that moment.

He quickly grabbed hold of Sabreena and sat her in a chair. He held her firmly as she sobbed and assured her that Evelyn was being helped. As he felt Sabreena calming and regaining her composure, he loosened his grip. Daniel offered Sabreena tissue to clean her face and then he spoke softly to her, "it's ok baby sis. We're going to be just fine. Everything is ok. She's not guilty and as soon as they can get her dramatic arse off of that floor, we're getting the hell out of this place for good and going to celebrate".

Daniel felt it safe to make light of the situation because he caught a glimpse, through the crowd, of Evelyn sitting up on the floor and talking to the medical personnel. It was over. They had survived abuse, addiction, the threat of incarceration and a multitude of other struggles that life had thrown at him. Daniel decided in that moment that he would protect his sisters with everything in him to keep them from suffering any other tragedies in life.

Daniel and Sabreena sat outside of the courthouse waiting for Evelyn and Aaron to join them. They joked about Evelyn reacting to the verdict. "She is going to hear my mouth about scaring me half to death! I can't believe she fainted. Not miss hold it together no matter what. You've got to be kidding me", Sabreena said jokingly as she imitated Evelyn falling into Aaron's arms.

"Wait, I know you're not talking. You were hyperventilating and snotting all over the place before I grabbed hold of you. Yelling across the court room like Celie and Nettie being kept apart. I didn't know whether to hold you or shake you", Daniel teased Sabreena as he shook his head laughing. "Shut up D! I thought Eve was having a damn heart attack. Shoot, I almost had one of my own", Sabreena jokingly said to Daniel.

Just then, a relieved and overjoyed Evelyn came marching out of the courthouse with a clearly confident Aaron. "Celebratory dinner at Eddie V's! My treat", Aaron announced as he approached Sabreena and Daniel. Then he looked over at Evelyn and whispered to her, "Remember what I said about my plans for your sister after you were free? I meant that. I need your help with something so be ready to help a brother out". Evenly smiled graciously and hugged Aaron and responded, "You already know little bro. I got ya back like you had mine. Really Aaron… I'm forever grateful for you".

"Alright, break it up! He's all mine now. You two have had your time. Now let's go eat! A sista is HUNGRY hungry", Sabreena said jokingly as she squeezed in between the two of them and locked her arms around each of their arms. They all laughed as they made their way to the lot to retrieve their cars. "Hey, do you mind if I ride in the car with Eve and D? I mean, I love your company, but I just want to be near Eve for a little while longer", Sabreena said charmingly to Aaron while batting her lashes.

"Get out of here little wolf. Go run with your pack", Aaron replied playfully as he placed a gentle kiss on her forehead before watching her walk off to catch up with her siblings. Aaron walked in the opposite direction to get his vehicle. He turned a corner and as he was approaching his car he stopped abruptly. He squinted to gain good focus. "You have got to be kidding me", Aaron said under his breath. As he was got closer, he became infuriated. Two of his tires were flattened. "Who the heck would have the guts to do this in the courthouse parking lot", Aaron spat out in frustration.

He shot Sabreena a text message: *"Hey, I have two flat tires. Probably some kind of retaliation from an old case. No worries. Order what I like, and I'll catch up shortly"*. Aaron called his roadside assistance to tow his car to the dealership. Once the tow truck took his car, he took a rideshare car service to the restaurant to catch up with Sabreena, Evelyn and Daniel. "Looks like I'm right on time", Aaron said as he arrived just as the food was being placed on the table. He knew Sabreena was a little uneasy about his tires being flattened, but they both opted to just enjoy the celebratory dinner and revisit the issue in their own time.

Daniel raised his glass of water and tapped on it gently with a butter knife. "Everyone, may I have your attention? Please raise your glasses of water to Eve for her tremendous show of strength and faith and to Aaron for his skills in the courtroom. I just want to raise a toast to you guys and send a humble thanks to Allah for the outcome. I'm glad to have my family back without the threat of losing one over our heads. May Allah continue to bless us with safekeeping. Salud", Daniel said before raising his glass to drink. "Salud", everyone else spoke in agreement before raising their glasses to drink.

Evelyn sent out her own praises of gratitude into the Universe as she ate and laughed and enjoyed her honorary celebration with those, she loved the most. In that moment she made a mental note to reach out to Marie, who was not doing well, after dinner. She observed the overflow of love and joy at that little table. She thought about the blessing extended to her today and she was excited to make the best of every moment of her life from that day forward. "Everything is well within me", she thought as she mentally joined the rest of the family again.

Proverbs 18:22

"Whoso findeth a wife findeth a good thing, and obtaineth favour of the Lord"

Aaron sat outside of Evelyn's home waiting patiently for her to come out. "D warned me that she's never on time", he thought to himself. Just as the thought crossed his mind, Evelyn walked out of the door. Aaron walked around to let her in his car and then closed the door behind her. As he walked around to the driver's side, he glanced across the street at a parked vehicle adjacent to him. He felt as if he had seen a ghost, but the tint on the windows was light enough to see inside but just dark enough to not really make out features clearly.

Aaron attempted to take a better look without being obvious, but the car pulled off before he could get a better look. He shrugged it off and got into his car. "You ok bro?", Evelyn asked with concern. "Huh? Oh...Yes. I'm okay sis", Aaron replied. He didn't realize that Evelyn was watching the entire time. "I thought I saw someone I knew, but I was mistaking", Aaron explained. "Ok then. Let's go find the perfect ring for our perfect pain in the butt", Evelyn said with excitement.

As they pulled off, Aaron's phone lit up. It was a call from a private number. Aaron answered through the speaker in his car, "Hello. Hello? Aaron here. Hello? I guess they don't want anything". Aaron disconnected the call, but as fast as he hung up the phone another private call came in. "Hello? Anyone there? I guess not", Aaron said as he disconnected the call. "It was probably a telemarketer", Evelyn said to break the tension. "Welp, whomever it was I guess they'll call back if it's important. I got stuff to do. Later for that". Aaron and Evelyn laughed it off and went about their plans.

"So, we're really driving all the way to Myrtle Beach to view Jacob the Jeweler's rings", Evelyn questioned. "Nope! A small collection is coming to me. We are meeting with a wealthy associate of mine with some serious connections. He owes me a favor and my baby is worth cashing in on it. I'm just hoping the options are good enough", Aaron explained proudly. Evelyn's face lit up with pure joy in response to the love that Aaron was expressing for her baby sister. She felt like she no longer needed to worry or hover over Sabreena's life since Aaron entered it, and that was a huge relief.

They drove for a good forty-five minutes before they slow rolled up a long and curvy driveway and stopped in front of a huge fancy gate with a camera call box. Aaron waited a few seconds before the gates slowly opened and he finished up the driveway and to the front of the beautiful estate home. "Wow little bro. You didn't say your friends had it like this! Is he single? Yeesh!", Evelyn said in awe. Aaron laughed in response to Evelyn's question as he walked around to help her out of the car. "Behave in here sis", Aaron said playfully as Evelyn got out of the car. "I will do my best", Evelyn said coyly as they both made their way to the enormous front doors.

Evelyn was in awe when the doors opened to a grand staircase with the most beautiful chandelier centered above it. They were escorted to an elegant sitting area with furniture that looked so rich, Evelyn felt the need to look to Aaron for permission to sit on it. The staff entered the room with two fancy rolling tables that contained multiple mock ring samples on them.

"I pulled out all the stops for my guy here. And who is this lovely lady with you; the bride to be?", Felix announced as he entered the room. Aaron stood, excitedly, to greet a tall, chiseled olive complected man with dark curly hair. "Felix, this is my sister-in-law to be, Evelyn. Evelyn, this is my good friend Felix". Aaron observed the two of them, sizing one another up. He cleared his throat to get their attention. "Man, this is quite a selection of rings. I don't even know where to start", Aaron said commanding the attention of his friend. "Why don't we let the beautiful lady decide", Felix replied without breaking his gaze at Evelyn.

Evelyn, now clearly blushing, turned her focus to the two tables and began to visually scan the selection. "This one is beautiful Aaron. Oh, and this one too. Wait… this one is absolutely Bree", Evelyn rattled on until Felix interrupted saying, "Evelyn, right? Let's model them for my guy here". Felix got down on one knee and placed one of Evelyn's choices on her ring finger. "What do you think Aaron? Isn't this a perfect choice", Felix asked while staring intently into Evelyn's eyes. "Uhhh… I think you two can flirt over lunch. Can we please decide on one of these beauties for my baby now? The surprise engagement party is less than a month away and the ring still needs to be crafted", Aaron replied.

"Alright. Alright. Let's give the baby a bottle so he can stop whining", Felix teased as he stood upright. Evelyn stood there awkwardly blushing and secretly impressed. She glanced down at the ring and her thoughts momentarily got away from her. She began to imagine her life there in that extravagant home with the beautiful and enticing Felix. Then she snapped back to reality to the sound of Aaron calling her name.

"Evelyn? Is that a yes, or no?", Aaron asked with the beautifully designed ring held in between his pointer and thumb. "Huh? Oh. Let me see. Wow! Ok, little brother! That is a beauty. The setting in that thing is gonna cost you your limbs. But that is DEFINITELY the one", Evelyn said with great excitement. In that moment, Evelyn was pulled in by the smells of something delightful. "I don't know what's on the menu Felix, but I'm definitely feeling like I want to kiss the cook right now! Whatever you have planned for lunch smells absolutely mouthwatering", Evelyn said while rubbing her stomach.

The guys laughed in unison at Evelyn as they all exited the room and made their way out to a beautiful terrace. Evelyn was yet again in awe at the beautiful landscaping surrounding the terrace. There was a round modest sized table covered in white linen and set with the top-of-the-line chinaware and silverware. Evelyn took her seat directly across from Felix and Aaron.

She took a good look at Felix while he and Aaron were engaged in conversation. She couldn't help but wonder how such a wealthy and handsome man could be single. "So, Felix, is being single your secret to looking so youthful? Wait… I'm not insinuating that you're old. I just… I meant… Oh gosh. I'm sorry if I'm offending you. It was really meant to come across as a compliment. Someone please say something and stop me from blabbing, please", Evelyn rattled off nervously.

Aaron decided to chime in and come to her rescue, "You're good sis, considering you're sitting at a table with two very seasoned attorneys. We habitually become silent when we sense someone squirming". Evelyn's face looked as if it lost all of its color. Evelyn nervously picked up her glass of water and began spoke into the glass, "You're not helping Aaron". Felix covered his face as he chuckled. He could sense Evelyn's embarrassment.

"Don't mind him, Evelyn. He found your sister and suddenly he's the man. I'm actually a widower. My wife passed away nine years ago. She had a very aggressive form of cancer. She was my childhood love and best friend. I lost the best parts of me when she died. I took some time to heal before I tried my hand at dating again. I felt like everyone I met was either looking for help or an evaluation away from a mental health diagnosis. It is scary out there.

I decided four years ago that I was better off single until God sends me someone who just feels right. My friends like to joke that my wife has put the brakes on my love life. Honestly speaking, she made me promise that I wouldn't spend the rest of my life alone. I just feel like alone and happy is much better than being miserable with the wrong person. So, I just enjoy my life one day at a time and maybe one day a beautiful woman will walk through my door with her brother-in-law to be and sweep me off of my feet. Maybe I'm just a helpless romantic with a wild imagination; because that could never happen to an ordinary guy like me", Felix finished explaining coyly with the most enticing smirk on his face.

"Ehh Hmm! Who are you today, Bro? For the love of my sanity, please give her your number and continue this conversation some other time. This is worse than me watching you lose in court. Eve, you are beet red. Don't tell me you're falling for this Casanova act", Aaron teased playfully. "Well, for what it's worth Felix, your wife sounds like she can never be replaced, only honored and respected. I'm sorry your time with her was not longer. I pray that you find the one that can at least compliment you in a way that she'd be pleased with", Evelyn said humbly.

"Thank you beautiful lady that walked through my door with her brother-in-law to be and – ", Felix was saying as he was abruptly interrupted by Aaron. "Oh, thank God! Look y'all. Lunch is being served". Felix threw up his hands and retorted, "The hate is so real. It be ya own friends". Everyone laughed as their plates were being placed in front of them. They didn't hesitate to dig in as they engaged in lighter conversation during lunch.

Felix gave them a tour of the rest of his home after lunch. Evelyn was blown away and grew very excited at the sight of his infinity pool. "You're welcome to come for a swim anytime Evelyn. Just make sure that you bring better company with you next time. This guy is a Debbie downer. So serious. What is he, a lawyer or something?", Felix said jokingly as they made their way back to exit the front of the home.

They said their goodbyes as the staff pulled up with Aaron's car. Felix rushed to escort Evelyn to the passenger side and opened her door. He slid his business card to her before winking smoothly and closing the door. "Aaron my guy, it's been a pleasure as usual. Evelyn, I hope to see you again", Felix said. Evelyn shot Felix back a slick wink in response as Aaron was pulling off. Evelyn started rattling off excitedly, "I'm so excited Bro! Now we just have to finalize the engagement party plans and figure out how to get Bree there. This is turning out to be the best year we've had in forever"!

"Something tells me that all of this excitement is not just about Bree and me. You really like Felix, huh? I saw him slip you that card too. Just be careful sis", Aaron said like an overly protected brother. "Oh gosh! Do you ever miss anything?! Bro, I'm ok. Really. I know you've grown so protective of me after weathering the trial with me; but I'm not as fragile as you all think. I have my moments, but I have made my peace with the way that everything happened. I know Troy had his demons, but it was no excuse to use me as a punching bag. That night, it was him or me; and I chose me. I will continue to choose me at all costs, and that is the last time I want to have to insist that I am fine", Evelyn replied firmly.

With that being said, Evelyn reached over and turned on the radio. Aaron opted to remain pleasantly silent for the rest of the ride. While he meant well, Evelyn had a way of drawing a line in the sand that even a well-seasoned attorney wouldn't dare cross. They arrived at Evelyn's home and Aaron thanked her for assisting him in making such a monumental decision in his life. "I'm sorry for being so snippy with you Aaron. I just want to move on with life. I want to get back to some sense of normal. I'm used to being the overbearing protective sibling, so I guess I was triggered. I know we've bonded over the trial, and you've become extra protective of me, but I promise you that I can take care of myself little brother", Evelyn said so sincerely.

Aaron replied apologetically, "I'm sorry sis. I don't even know why I was so bothered by Felix and you flirting. He's actually a really great guy. He doesn't care how lonely it gets; he'd just rather be alone if it isn't the right woman. Now that I think about it, you two are probably perfect for each other. I know you don't need my permission, but for what it's worth I wouldn't object to it sis". Evelyn, tickled at Aaron going on and on replied, "Thanks counselor. I appreciate the green light. And for what it's worth; I am so relieved that it is you that's taking Sabreena off my hands permanently. I didn't think she'd ever submit to love. You're a great guy too Aaron. I'm honored to be your future sister-in-law. Now let me out of this car before I start crying and snotting all over the place".

They both laughed in unison as Aaron made his way around to let Evelyn out of the car. He walked Evelyn to the door and gave her a brotherly hug goodbye. "Just make sure you can take care of her after paying for that ring, because ain't no givebacks! You're stuck with her", Evelyn said jokingly. "Ha ha ha! You got jokes. Our girl isn't that bad, she just needed a brotha with a backbone", Aaron retorted through his laughs. He saw Evelyn inside safely and then went on his way. Aaron couldn't help but smile from ear to ear the entire ride home. He was so in love with everything about Sabreena and he couldn't wait to do right by her. He felt today was a prelude to the greatest chapter of his life and he cruised all the way home in his feelings.

Ephesians 6:11,12

"11 Put on the whole armour of God, that ye may be able to stand against the wiles of the devil. 12 For we wrestle not against flesh and blood, but against principalities, against powers, against the rulers of the darkness of this world, against spiritual wickedness in high places". Ephesians 6: 11,12

Evelyn was excited about her plans with Felix today. It had been nearly two weeks since their introduction. After a week, Evelyn could not stop thinking about him. She decided to casually reach out and the two of them had been in touch regularly ever since. Evelyn woke up to a text message from Felix that read: ***"Good morning beautiful. I hope you slept well. I am sending a car for you, as I will be wrapping up some business while you're on your way to me. The driver will arrive promptly at noon. I look forward to seeing you again. I will make sure to exceed any of your expectations. See you soon angel face".***

As cheesy as they sounded at times, Evelyn could not get enough of Felix's pet names for her. It had been quite some time since anyone had doted on her this way.

Melancholy memories of Troy crept into her mind but was quickly shrugged away at her will. Evelyn continued her ritualistic morning routine. No one was aware of the deep changes that overtook Evelyn after awakening from her coma. They just knew she seemed more grounded in every way.

Evelyn went into one of the spare rooms that she had recently transformed into a Zen space. She sat comfortably in front of her prayer alter and lit a white candle that was placed in a crystal-clear lotus shaped candle holder. She then lit a bundle of sage and the stick of Palo Santo wood that was place beside the sage in an elevated decorative seashell. Evelyn broke the silence with five even paced strikes to her sound bowl. She waited to feel the sensation of her energy rising and with closed eyes, she let her body relax as he took a few deep breaths.

Inhaling and exhaling for a few exchanges, Evelyn released any tension she may have been holding. Then she permeated the atmosphere with a beautiful melodic chant, "nam myoho renge kyo, nam myoho renge kyo, nam myoho renge kyo". Evelyn could do this for hours on any given day, as the rhythmic and melodic chanting soothed every corner of her soul and brought her indescribable comfort. However, today she knew she had to be mindful of her time, so she narrowed to an hour.

Feeling centered and full of excitement, Evelyn proceeded to get herself ready for her lunch date with Felix. "Where the heck is my make-up pouch", Evelyn said aloud as she tore through the surfaces in her bathroom looking. Just then, she remembered that she carried out with her yesterday and tucked it under the front passenger seat of her car. She scurried down the stairs and grabbed her keys as she made her way out of the door. She took a few steps in the direction of her car and stopped abruptly while grabbing her chest and stumbling backwards in disbelief

"What the holy hell is this?! What...Why... Oh my GOD! Are you kidding me right now?!", Evelyn shouted into the air. Evelyn was thrown into shock from what she was seeing. Every panel of her vehicle was carved into with derogatory slurs, directed at her. All four of her tires were flattened and there was a brick that was place on the hood, wrapped in a piece of paper that read, "This is your final warning.

Your house is next. Learn your place or be put in it!".

Evelyn's adrenaline rushed through her as she took this all in. She was sure that this was the work of one of Troy's angry family members but couldn't be sure who would have the nerve to take it this far. She immediately contacted the police, then she texted Felix to cancel their plans. She reached out to Daniel and Sabreena to catch them up to speed. Of course, the two of them were enroute to her before she could even hang up with them.

As Evelyn waited for the police to arrive, she thought back over the last two weeks. She realized in an instant that the strange string of events that had been happening were all related to and leading up to this. She didn't pay it any mind at the time, but over the last couple of weeks she'd encountered a dead cat on her lawn, a broken floodlight bulb on the side of her house, feces on her lawn that she now shuttered to think of whether it was from a person or a dog, and a single dead rose that was left under her vibrantly growing rose bush.

She was sure to report all of these happenings to the officers when they arrived to take her report. As the officers were leaving, Daniel and Sabreena were pulling into the driveway. Daniel's jaw dropped in disbelief at the sight of Evelyn's vehicle. Sabreena's face turned beet red as the expression of pure rage took over her face. "Who do I need to see about this Eve?! Tell me now and I'm on my way", Sabreena exclaimed in anger.

"Calm down Bree. Let the police do their job", Evelyn replied in a very calm manner. "Hell to the NO! I'm out for blood over my big sis. They want war then I will bring it to their front door. And how are you so poised right now? Why aren't you making calls to them low lives", Sabreena snapped back angrily. Evelyn put her hand to her forehead and took a deep breath. She replied, "I don't know who did this Bree. I can't just go accusing people without having facts. I know this is as frustrating for you as it is for me, but don't worry. I've prayed about it and left it there. I can't give this anymore energy. I have to contact my insurance company and get this car out of my driveway before the neighbors get the wrong idea".

Sabreena drew her neck back and nearly rolled her eyes out of her head before replying, "Screw these neighbors! And Screw Troy's family! Screw all of this! D, take me home to get some things because when they come back, I'll be camped out and waiting. It's gonna be a swinging bat straight from the door type of situation too. That's on everything I love"!

Sabreena made her way aggressively out of the door while still rambling on about how she was going to bring it if someone dared to return to Evelyn's home. "Uhhh, I guess I'll be right back with little miss fire starter", Daniel said reluctantly as he made his way out of the door behind Sabreena. Evelyn just waived her hands in the air to signal her indifference to it all as she dialed Felix's number to respond to his numerous inquisitive text messages.

Evelyn let the phone ring until his voicemail picked up. She declined to leave a message, assuming he'd call back when he could. As Sabreena and Daniel were ready to pull off from the driveway, Daniel's car was blocked in by an oversized SUV with tinted windows. "What the heck is this? Excuse us! Why are you blocking us in?", Sabreena yelled from the open window. The rear door of the SUV opened, and Felix stepped out. He smiled pleasantly and responded, "I apologize young lady. You must be Sabreena. I'm - -".

"Felix? Wha... What are you doing here", Evelyn shouted in confusion from her doorway. "You know this guy, Eve? Are you a detective or something, sir? Because I don't need backup! These people got me feeling froggy. I want somebody to come back here with the nonsense because they'll get exactly what they're looking for", Sabreena ranted. "Bre calm down!", Daniel and Evelyn shouted in unison. They'd had enough of Sabreena's fiery rant. "Who are you, sir? You're calling out my government name like you know me, sooo...", Sabreena responded unphased by her siblings' scolding.

Evelyn made her way down the driveway, still confused at Felix's presence. A flatbed truck pulled up behind Felix's ride as she reached Felix. "Felix, what are you doing here? Is this tow truck with you?", Evelyn questioned. Felix nodded in the affirmative. Evelyn continued, "How'd you know what was going on? Wait…let me guess. Sabreena filled Aaron in on her way here and you called Aaron when I didn't respond to your calls or texts, then he filled you in. So, here you are".

Felix never even raised an eyebrow in the midst of all that was going on. Just like a well composed lawyer, he waited patiently to speak. "Well, I was a bit worried. So yes, I called Aaron. Once he filled me in, I ordered a tow truck to your home, and I've arranged for it to be taken to the body shop. I've left specific instructions for them to contact me for payment when the repairs are done. I've also arranged for one of the cars in my car service to standby here for your daily transportation needs until you get your car back", Felix explained.

"Well Damn stranger. Anything else?!", Sabreena interrupted. "Sabreena!", Daniel and Evelyn spat in unison once again. Felix let out a warm laugh through looks of admiration at the obvious closeness of the three siblings. He spoke again, breaking the tension, "Hi, I'm Felix. I'm good friends with Aaron and he introduced me to Evelyn. It's nice to finally meet you in person Sabreena. He's told me so much about you".

Sabreena folded her arms and retorted, "well I've never even heard of you. But it's very nice to meet you too Felix. Okaaay Eve. Somebody DEFINITELY got her groove baaack with this one", Sabreena said through a coy smirk while cutting her eyes over at Evelyn. Evelyn shook her head and pointed in the direction of Daniel's car. "Bye Bree. I will see you two when you get back", Evelyn said firmly while shooting Daniel a stern look, as if to say he'd better get Sabreena and get on his way. "Yeah, yeah, yeah. I've been kicked out of worse places Sissy. You kiddos better behave while I'm gone too. I got my eye on you Mr. Felix", Sabreena teased as she got in the car.

Felix was so tickled just watching them interact. "Felix, you didn't have to do all of this. I'm so grateful for your help and your swift response to all of this. You know my insurance would have covered this, right?", Evelyn said. "Yes Beautiful. I'm aware. I just didn't want you to have to go through the trouble of it all. Besides, it's only money. I can't take it with me so I should spend it thoughtfully while I'm still here", Felix replied. "Felix, I'm sorry all of this happened today of all days. I hope it wasn't too much trouble having to cancel whatever plans you had for us. I just feel like a whole burden today", Evelyn said sorrowfully.

"Just like an angel to be apologetic about something that wasn't even their fault. You're an amazing soul Evelyn. I could never view you as a burden. Besides, I made arrangements for a jazz band to play in my courtyard while we enjoyed lunch. The offer is still on the table if you want to just take your mind off all this and enjoy yourself for a bit", Felix replied kindly. "I think I will take you up on that offer Felix. I just need to clear my head. Sabreena has her own key, so I'm sure she will let herself in when she comes back. A change of scenery with a handsome man is exactly what I need after all this excitement", Evelyn replied flirtatiously. Felix, grinning from ear to ear, waited for Evelyn to lock up. He extended his arm and escorted her to the truck. He joined her and off they went to make the best of what started as an eventful day.

Felix had outdone himself. Evelyn was blown away by the outside décor as well as the food selection. The band playing in the background was the perfect touch to set the mood. The two of them laughed, ate, talked and ate some more. Evelyn forgot all about her tumultuous morning. She felt like everything about Felix was too good to be true. Nonetheless, she was grateful to have come across such a great man after everything she'd survived.

In the midst of their interaction, Evelyn breathed in deeply and gave a silent thanks as she exhaled. She shrugged off the thought at first, but eventually she allowed herself to imagine the possibility of having a life with Felix. "Why not me? I'm just as good of a choice as anyone", Evelyn thought. She could feel an emotional overflow rushing through her as she allowed herself to be accepting of that thought. Just thinking about it left her in the most peaceful space for the rest of that day.

John 15:13

13 Greater love hath no man than this, that a man lay down his life for his friends.

Aaron could not seem to keep his cool this morning. Everything just had to be perfect. He picked up Sabreena's ring the day before and tossed and turned the entire night. It was the most beautiful symbol of his love that he'd ever laid eyes on, but to him it couldn't be compared to the beauty that Sabreena possessed, inside and out. Aaron called Evelyn to make sure the venue was set up to his satisfaction and direct instructions.

"Really little bro? You're micromanaging me? I have everything under control. I'm on my way to pick up Marie from her treatment. Daniel is at the venue waiting for the food, beverages and the pastries. Sabreena has no clue what's going on. She thinks we are celebrating Daniel's sobriety. The DJ was arriving to set up when I was pulling off", Evelyn rattled off.

"Are you sure Sabreena hasn't figured it out? She was questioning my whereabouts yesterday when I drove out to get the ring from Felix. That woman should've been a detective because she is a bloodhound", Aaron exclaimed. Evelyn, laughing hysterically, assured Aaron that Sabreena was clueless about the engagement and that everything was under control.

Evelyn pulled up to the treatment center and found Marie sitting on a bench outside in her Sunday best. "Ok Marie. I see you. You are sharp", Evelyn teased as Marie stood with her cane and did a little half twirl. Evelyn assisted Marie into the car and off they went to meet Sabreena. "I can't tell you how grateful to God that I am to be alive and well enough to see my baby girl get proposed to. I know Sabreena and I always butt heads, but I love her so dearly and I prayed for the day to see you all happy and well off", Marie confessed through teary eyes and a shaky voice.

Evelyn reached into her arm console and pulled out a few tissues. She handed them over to Marie and replied, "Ok now Marie, this is a happy day. We are not going to be weirdly emotional around Sabreena. So, get it out of your system before we get to her because you know that girl picks up on everything". Marie and Evelyn chuckled as Marie wiped her face. "That child has been alert and aware to everything happening around her since the day she was born. Looking around the labor room like she had questions, only minutes old", Marie responded through a lighthearted laugh.

Evelyn replied, "Aaron said she was poking around at his absence last night when he went to get her ring. That girl is relentless. I have to be honest. I am going to love the look of surprise on her face when she realizes this was all for her. You know she's going to be a little upset that she didn't figure it out beforehand, right?" Marie, still chuckling, shook her head in agreement. They gained their composure as they arrived at Sabreena's home. "Sit tight Marie. I'll go put a rush on the lady of the hour", Evelyn said as she exited the vehicle.

"Bree. Breeee!", Evelyn called out as she knocked on the door aggressively. The door flung open, "Ummm. HELLO! Police?! Like, what the heck Eve?!", Sabreena said clearly annoyed at her sister knocking and yelling. "Oh hush! Hurry up slow poke. I got Marie sitting in the car, waiting", Evelyn snapped back. Sabreena was just about to say something sassy in regard to Marie waiting, but she decided to just hold her tongue and pick up her pace.

Evelyn shot Sabreena a warning stare as she turned to walk back to the car, as if to tell Sabreena to be mindful of her time. Sabreena rolled her eyes with reluctancy but made sure to keep up with her faster pace. She finished applying her lipstick and tossed it in her bag. She heard a light horn tap as she grabbed her jacket. "Ok! I'm coming now! Sheesh", Sabreena screeched as she walked out the door and closed and locked it behind her.

Sabreena joined Evelyn and Marie and they were not even 5 minutes down the road before the friction between Sabreena and Marie reared its ugly head. "Marie, I'm sure you didn't mind waiting for me to come out. How many years did we wait for Marie to return Eve? I lost count after I graduated from high school", Sabreena said childishly. "Bree, What the hell?!", Evelyn spat at Sabreena. "No…no, it's ok. Let her get it all out before we get to where we are going. It's not enough that any day can be my last. This child of mine just wants to stop the clock on me right this very moment", Marie said defensively.

"Yeah. Right. Because you're the victim Marie. YOU, YOU, YOU! God forbid you let anybody else be in that seat",

Sabreena said bitterly. Evelyn pulled the car over on the side of the road and took a few deep breaths. "Oh Lord! Now we gotta wait for Ghandi to get herself together", Sabreena said coldly. "What the entire hell is your problem Sabreena", Evelyn exclaimed. Sabreena, now looking like a toddler caught red handed with snacks, just stared at Evelyn as if she was in shock.

"No! No! Don't look at me that way. We are going to put these childish antics to rest, and we are gonna put this to rest right now! I am sick to death of you turning every family event into your own personal death match. So, spill it! Whatever it is that you haven't let go, let it out. Because God knows EVERYBODY is tired of walking on eggshells when it comes to you. You want firecracker Eve? You got her! The gloves are off baby sis! Let's go!", Evelyn yelled at Sabreena while flailing her arms like a mad woman.

The car was silent for a good ten seconds and then Marie burst into laughter. Sabreena, breaking her deep stare at Evelyn, began to laugh uncontrollably as well. Now it was Evelyn who looked confused. "Are you two kidding me right now! Unbelievable! It's no wonder the two of you fight like cats and dogs. You're just alike. Immature with a sense of humor. How is this even remotely funny? And who the HELL are you calling Sabreena?!", Evelyn said in a rage.

"Well. If you must know. I'm calling Aaron so that he can call Felix and we can set up a booty call for you, because CLEARLY someone needs to release some tension around here", Sabreena said arrogantly. Evelyn placed her head in her hands and took a few more deep breaths. She looked up again to see Sabreena and Marie both still snickering. "You two are impossible. I just want to get to this party and get the heck away from the both of you right now. I am so over you two", Evelyn rattled on as she pulled off. Everyone was wise to keep silence for the remainder of the ride.

They pulled up to the courtyard of the country club and Sabreena was blown away by the beautiful decorations. "Wow! This is pretty fancy for a man's sobriety party. Something y'all wanna tell me? Is D making a special announcement about his lifestyle today", Sabreena said jokingly. Evelyn and Marie glanced at each other with the secret they were keeping in mind. They

all made their way into the courtyard
together to join the party that seemed to just
have started.

Midway through the tables Marie
announced, "This is close enough ladies. I
can't walk any further. These legs of mine
are gonna sit and rest right here while you
kids... how do they say it these days???
Turn up", Marie said through a cheerful
laugh. Evelyn and Sabreena sat their
belongings down at the table with Marie and
continued towards the platform stage to join
Daniel.

Daniel saw them approaching and
waved for them to come to him. "Congrats
D! This is beautiful. I'm so proud of you",
Sabreena said as she embraced her brother.
Daniel and Evelyn kept Sabreena busy as
the guests began to arrive and fill up the
seats far in the back as instructed. Aaron did
not want Sabreena catching on to the fact
that her closest friends were in attendance.

The three of them danced and
laughed in a group together just like when
they were children. Marie watched from
afar with tears of joy swelling in her eyes.
They were having so much fun together that
none of them were even aware of Felix and
Aaron making their entrance and pulling

down the banner to set the stage in preparation for the big question. They always had a way of appearing to be only amongst themselves, even in a room full of people.

Their playful dancing was abruptly interrupted by the sound of Aaron's voice coming over the microphone. "Attention everyone. I just want to thank you all for coming out tonight to celebrate with the family on this special and joyous occasion", Aaron began. Sabreena looked confused. "Why is he down there acting like he's the MC of the party or something? He just has to have the courtroom's attention at all times", Sabreena said sounding agitated.

Aaron continued, "As you all know, I've been friends with the family for a while now. Tragedy turned triumphant is our story. I am so glad that Marie chose me to assist in that victory for such a beautiful soul as Evelyn's. Since that victory, I have had the pleasure of being a brother to Eve and D, and I would like to think that Marie sees me as a son since I AM dating her beautiful daughter Bree".

Sabreena, now really confused, began to zoom in on the crowd and she noticed a few of her friends scattered about.

She thought quickly, "why would they be here for D's party"? Just as the thought crossed her mind, Aaron made his way up to the platform where Sabreena was standing and he continued to speak, "Speaking of my beautiful Sabreena... Bree, you are both a breath of fresh air and the swift kick that sends it flying. Wait...that sounded a little better when I practiced it. Anyway. You're the first thing I think about in the morning when I rise and the last thing I think about before falling asleep at night. You are what I dream about all night in between. I can't imagine a life without you in it and I'm not even sure how I thought life was remotely ok before you came into mine",

Just then, Aaron pulled a black velvet box out of his pocket and got down on one knee. The crowd gasped as he opened the box to reveal the beautiful ring enclosed. Sabreena, in full shock and with tears rolling down her face, now stared in awe at the ring and then back at Aaron in disbelief. Aaron continued, "Sabreena Williams, I don't want to just think of you day and night. I don't just want to dream of you night after night. I want you beside me as my wife and best friend. I stand here before every watching, professing my undying lo - -". "Oh my God! Yes! Yes

Aaron. I will marry you! This is NOT a closing argument baby! Puleeez put that ring on this finger and kiss me already", Sabreena interrupted.

The entire room burst out in laughter as Aaron, smiling and shaking his head, placed the ring on Sabreena's finger with an insurmountable amount of joy. He stood and grabbed Sabreena tight, lifting and swinging her around as he kissed her in celebration. Aaron, with his chest puckered, grabbed the mic and shouted, "Aye DJ! She said yes! Play our song". The bass dropped and everyone took to the dance floor dancing to the sound of Jagged Edge's So So Def Remix "Let's Get Married".

Pure bliss is what everyone seemed to be wearing on their faced as the laughed and danced in celebration. Marie was crying like a baby while dancing along in her chair. She couldn't help but notice a young lady standing a few feet from her in dark shades and what looked like a bob cut wig. The young lady appeared to be clinched at the jaw and was not celebrating with everyone else. Marie tried to wave and shout aloud to grab the woman's attention over the music, but it was no use because the music was way too loud.

As she grabbed her cane and made her way over to check on the strange woman, she noticed that the woman was holding something in her right hand. Marie walked a little closer, now focused on the woman's hand. Her jaw dropped as she was right up on the woman when she raised her hand, aiming it with a gun in it directly at Sabreena. "Sweet Jesus, please help us", Marie yelled out as she threw her body in front of the woman at the same time that a single gunshot rang out.

The entire crowed reacted immediately in chaos. Some went running and others hit the floor. "Call 911, Call 911", people were yelling in the midst of all of the confusion. Aaron, who had covered Sabreena with his own body was now looking up to see what he could make of things. As he scanned the crowd in motion, he saw Marie laying still in a puddle of blood and the mysterious woman running from the courtyard. "Dear God, this can't be happening. Tell me my eyes are deceiving me", Daniel said under his breath as he jumped up and sprang over to Marie.

He rolled her over and began grabbing tablecloths and linen napkins to place over Marie's wound, but the bleeding was soaking them so fast, it seemed pointless. Aaron cried and called out to God for help as he frantically pushed the linens onto the wound and watched fearfully as they continued to be soaked through and through with blood. The sirens blazed in the distance as everyone looked on in shock.

Aaron seemed to be moving in shock as he desperately grabbed the linens from helping hands and tried to aimlessly to stop the profuse bleeding. Marie, eyes still closed, managed to find the strength to mutter in a shallow breath, "Sabreena". Cries and statements of disbelief echoed throughout the courtyard as the red and white lights reflected off of the walls. There were cops everywhere controlling the scene. The paramedics loaded Marie onto their rig and onlookers watched as the doors closed and the lights and sirens drifted off to the distance.

Aaron, covered in blood, finally laid his eyes on a weeping Sabreena. He rushed over to her, and she just collapsed in his arms. Everything seemed to stand still as everyone, clearly shaken up, was being instructed to remain on the scene for questioning. "It's the curse. It's the curse. It's the curse", Evelyn repeated in shock.

She was so far gone that she couldn't hear
Daniel pleading for them to get in the
officer's car so that they could rush to the
hospital. Felix tried to calm Evelyn down
with an embrace, but it was no use.
Everything seemed to have gone straight to
hell in the blink of an eye and as usual, they
never even saw it coming.

Matthew 5:4

4 Blessed are they that mourn: for they shall be comforted.

"I still don't understand why you've been so tight lipped with me Aaron. My mother was murdered by a strange woman and instead of the detectives reaching out to me and my siblings, they keep calling you in to talk to them. What are you not telling me Aaron?! And don't give me no crap about an ongoing investigation because I am way too smart for that. And I know this isn't about Eve's case because nobody has contacted Eve either. I want answers today or this wedding is off, and I am done. We haven't been keeping secrets and we are not going to start now", Sabreena exclaimed.

"Sabreena, baby. Please. I am really begging you to give me time to get you all of the right answers. I loved Marie like she was my own mother. Believe me, when I'm able to disclose any information to you, I will. But Sabreena you have to understand that I have to follow the rules with this. This is serious. I know you don't like being kept in the dark and believe me, I want more than anything to tell you what's going on. But the detectives are telling me that I just can't do that yet. Please tell me you understand that Bree", Aaron pleaded.

"Aaron, today I have to bury my mother without any answers. So, here's the deal. You can think about what those detectives said, or you can consider what I am saying. It's no longer up for discussion or negotiation Counselor. After that casket is lowered into the ground today, I need answers. No answers. No Sabreena and Aaron", Sabreena retorted.

"Oh my God, baby. Are you serious right now? My hands are tied Bree. Please don't do this! I am begging you", Aaron pleaded once again. But it was no use. Once Sabreena made up her mind, there was no changing it. She flagged Aaron off and made her way down to the family car that was waiting outside. Aaron grabbed his blazer and chased behind Sabreena. He caught up to her as she was walking out of the door and grabbed her gently by the wrist. Sabreena gave him a stern look before shaking loose from his hold. "I said what I said Aaron", she said firmly before leaving Aaron in the doorway.

Aaron followed shortly after, feeling torn and defeated. He knew she was not playing, and he felt as if his life was unraveling, and he couldn't do anything about it. The ride to the church was silent and uncomfortable. Aaron prayed to God that Sabreena would have a change of heart before the day was over, because what he was not disclosing was sure to stir their foundation. Sabreena was no fool and her intuition was telling her that she needed to get the facts before going any further with Aaron.

The church was filled that day and Daniel did not hesitate to point out to his sisters that Marie built a family with these people but could not bring herself to build one with them. He felt so conflicted in that moment. He realized that he had never resolved these feelings and deep cutting issues with Marie, and now he would never be able to. He looked up at the pulpit and had mixed emotions towards Aaron, as Aaron was giving Marie's eulogy. He felt as if Aaron had more of a mother and son relationship with Marie than he did. This revelation was cutting him deep at the most inconvenient time. He wanted to be the one up there speaking, but he and his sisters decided unanimously that Aaron was the best choice. He was in his head so much that Evelyn had to tap him after asking him twice to hand her a bible.

Daniel broke free from his thoughts and handed Evelyn a community bible. He said a silent prayer as the church prepared to read Marie's favorite scripture. "Ya Allah. Please purify my heart and restore in me, honor love and respect for the woman who gave me life. Ameen".

He tuned in as the church read aloud from the book of Luke, chapter 11 verses 1-10:

[1] And it came to pass, that, as he was praying in a certain place, when he ceased, one of his disciples said unto him, Lord, teach us to pray, as John also taught his disciples.

[2] And he said unto them, When ye pray, say, Our Father which art in heaven, Hallowed be thy name. Thy kingdom come. Thy will be done, as in heaven, so in earth.

[3] Give us day by day our daily bread.

[4] And forgive us our sins; for we also forgive every one that is indebted to us. And lead us not into temptation; but deliver us from evil.

[5] And he said unto them, Which of you shall have a friend, and shall go unto him at midnight, and say unto him, Friend, lend me three loaves;

[6] For a friend of mine in his journey is come to me, and I have nothing to set before him?

[7] And he from within shall answer and say, Trouble me not: the door is now shut, and my children are with me in bed; I cannot rise and give thee.

[8] I say unto you, Though he will not rise and give him, because he is his friend, yet because of his importunity he will rise and give him as many as he needeth.

[9] And I say unto you, Ask, and it shall be given you; seek, and ye shall find; knock, and it shall be opened unto you.

[10] For everyone that asketh receiveth; and he that seeketh findeth; and to him that knocketh it shall be opened.

"Amen and Amen. Thank you everyone. Sister Marie would have been pleased. We will now hear a selection from the choir as we exit the church and align for the procession to the burial plot", The pastor announced.

As the family and friends made their way to the cemetery to lay Marie to rest, Daniel noticed that the bright and sunny skies began to look overcast. He didn't want to think anything of it, so he quickly dismissed his thoughts and tried to let the smooth jazz playing lightly through the speakers, carry his thoughts into a more peaceful space.

Evelyn rested on Felix's shoulder for both physical and emotional comfort, but Sabreena and Aaron were visibly in discord. As the car pulled up to the burial plot, Daniel felt overcome with anxiety. He was doing his very best to hold it together for his sisters, but they seemed to be handling their emotions a lot better than him. He led them and the other guest to form a circle around the burial site as he made a special space for Marie's fellow choir member to sing one of Marie's favorite gospel songs; Take Me to The King, by Tamela Mann.

Daniel and his sisters assisted each other in handing out the roses to be placed atop Marie's casket for her final goodbye. Marie's good friend Carol began singing in the most beautiful melodic tones and in an instant, the clouds opened up and let out a gentle rain in unison with the sun's brightly beaming rays. Daniel began to weep, releasing what he thought he'd be able to hold for a mor private moment. Evelyn and Sabreena took to each side of them with tears rolling down their faces.

Suddenly, a vibrant rainbow appeared so close that it felt like they could reach out and touch it. A single clap of thunder rang out and just as Carol was wrapping up the song. Daniel couldn't contain himself at the thought of what was happening. Sabreena pulled him closer to her and said low enough for only him and Evelyn to hear, "This is just like Marie. She always gotta be dramatic and have the last say", Sabreena said softly; attempting to take some of the weight off of Daniel's heavy heart.

The three of them chuckled through tear-soaked faces as they watched their mother being lowered into the ground. Arm in arm, the made their way back to the family car. Just like Marie's last glimpse of them, they were in a world of solitude that they'd created over the years for their own healing and comfort. It was as if the rest of the world had to wait for them to feel safe enough to reemerge.

Aaron and Felix took up closely behind them, both silently showing recognition and approval of their bond and their way. Aaron had a brief moment of discomfort when he remembered Sabreena's threat, but he decided to pray and release it and just be in the moment. He knew that things were going to be what they were gonna be, so he just prayed to weather the storm that he could foresee coming.

Nahum 1:7

The LORD is good, A stronghold in the day of trouble, And He knows those who take refuge in Him.

Felix stood at Aarons door, ringing the bell repeatedly while speaking into the doorbell camera, "Bro! Come to the door. I know you can hear this bell and me yelling! Open the door man. Evelyn won't let me rest until I send her visual proof of you being alive and ok. Listen! I will come through one of these windows before I go back to that woman empty handed. So, come down and open the- -", Aaron opened the door before Felix could finish threatening.

"Man, when is the last time you showered? The smell hit me before I stepped in. And is that mold on the pizza? How long has that box been sitting there? Awe, come on my guy! You're goin' out bad. I can't FaceTime Eve with you looking like this", Felix was in the middle of his rant when he turned to see his good friend with his head in the palms of his hands, silently sulking. Despite the smell, Felix mustered up the strength to sit next to Aaron. "Damn, you really got it bad Bro. I'm here. Give me the rundown", Felix said.

Aaron began to explain with tears running down his face, "It was Vanessa, or whatever her real name may be. She was behind everything. The flat tires on my car. The damage to Eve's car. The dead animals on the lawn. Man, she was the one who shot and killed Marie. The detectives told me that they have no clue as to her whereabouts. I explained it all to Sabreena and she lost it. She just kept throwing the word wife around. I tried to explain that the marriage was never legal, but before I could explain everything, she threw the ring at me and left. She won't answer her door or her phone. I've sent messages with roses and even tried to email an explanation. I can't breathe without her, man. It's been weeks. I can't function at all. I don't want a life without her in it. Our wedding date is a week away! I have to get her back Bro", Aaron went on in a panic.

Felix listened carefully before responding, "Ok. Listen. One thing at a time. You go take a shower. A looong shower. I'm going to clean up a little down here. I've sent a request for one of my cleaners to come and deep clean your place. We need to get you together my friend". Felix led Aaron to the stairs and began tidying up. An hour later, Aaron came down looking like a new man on the outside. "Come on. Let's get out of her way while she whips your place back into shape. We can talk this out over a meal... my treat", Felix said as he coached Aaron out of the door.

They sat down at a local Pub and Felix listened intently as Aaron poured his broken heart out. "Ok, I need you to go home and collect your thoughts. Sit down and write Bree a letter explaining everything and don't waste an opportunity to tell her how you really feel. I'm going to catch Eve up and see what she can do with Bree on her end. I will come by and grab the letter from you in the morning and drop it off to Eve. Once Eve softens up to the idea of just hearing you out via your letter, let's just all hope and pray she can see things from your perspective. So, choose your words wisely brother, because I feel like you only gonna get one shot at this", Felix explained.

Aaron seemed to have a ray of hope in his eyes after his talk with Felix. Aaron later sat in deep thought about everything he wanted to express to Sabreena. He closed his eyes and prayed harder than he'd ever prayed before. He wanted the influence of God and every Angel in his corner to assist

him with the right words in this letter.
Feeling like he had the help of God himself,
he sat there and poured everything out in his
letter to Sabreena:

Dear Sabreena,

*It was never my intent to hurt you
or blindside you in any way. Please believe
me when I say that I have never in my
entire life, laid eyes on a more perfect
woman than you. I love everything about
you, inside and out. I am an honest and
loyal man, but I am not flawless. I am
human and I make mistakes, and this was
one of them. I am begging you to forgive
me and to just give me a chance to explain.
If you are still reading, then I believe that
my cries out to God to bring you back to me
are being answered.*

*Sabreena, listen to me carefully.
That woman was never legally my wife. I
don't even know her true name til' this day.
She entered my life at a time where I'd lost
so much, and she was like a God send to
me; or so I thought. She weaseled her way
into my life with all the right lies. She
played on my emotions, and before I knew
it, I was in love with every lie that she had
fed to me, from her name to her
personality. I eventually proposed to her,*

and we got married. It wasn't long before my funds were being syphoned from my accounts and slowly being sent to an offshore account.

I didn't catch it right away. In fact, I would have probably never caught it because she managed the bills and finances. My bank alerted me when she got too greedy and attempted to transfer an amount that triggered an alert. She knew I was alerted and was already planning to take what she could and leave. Sabreena, I know this all sounds unreal so you can imagine how it felt to actually experience this. The story gets crazier. I rushed home to speak with her that day. I just could not bring myself to believe that my life was twisting and turning in such a way.

I came in the house that evening in a rush, searching and calling for her room by room. I reached the bedroom and saw the open suitcase and the already packed bags. Then I glanced across the room and saw a half-opened bag full of money. I paused in shock for a moment then made my way over to the bag. As I opened the bag the rest of the way and sifted through the wads of money, I felt something hard and heavy crack me in the back of my head. She attacked me and left me to die, bleeding from my skull all over the bedroom floor. If we had not scheduled the cleaning service to come that day, no one would have found me in time, and I would have likely died on that floor that day.

I won't get into the long process of legalities that took place after I was released from the hospital. I'll just tell you that my marriage to her was not legal. She had done this kind of thing, before targeting me. She got a pretty good head start since I was unconscious for three days and could not answer any questions explaining what happened or where she was. By the time I was questioned, she was long gone with no trace of where she'd gone. Sabreena; God is my witness, I haven't seen or heard from that woman in seven years. I honestly hoped her for dead but just prayed she was smart enough to never come near me again. It took a few years in therapy to treat my PTSD and the last few after that, I spent trying to forget that part of my life altogether. I really don't like to think or speak of it.

I truly understand why you're so pissed with me, believe me. But I swear to you that it was never my intent to hide anything from you or mislead you in any way. I was just happy to let someone in my life after being so guarded for so long. In some strange way, I truly believe that I blocked my experience with her completely from my mind while simultaneously building walls around me because of her. I really can't explain it, nor do I want to make excuses. It was careless of me to not have addressed it and I accept full responsibility for my error. I pray that we can speak face to face and get past this and get to a beautiful life together.

So, this is my final plea to you. I pray with everything in me that if I don't hear from you before our wedding date, that you take a chance on me and just show up. I pray that you believe in our love and its ability to conquer all. I pray that you believe in the fact that you just being you gave me the courage to open my heart up fully again. I don't want to imagine a life without you, and I will fight to get things back the way they were with us. I just pray that you give me the chance, Sabreena. I will be at that alter like we planned and I'm going to have faith that you see the greatness and the Divinity in this connection and show up too. Sabreena, please come back to me. I promise I will spend a lifetime showing you that it was worth it.

All My Love!

Aaron

Aaron sealed the letter and decided to call it a night. He allowed thoughts of Bree returning to him and all being well between them, fill his thoughts before drifting off to sleep.

Proverbs 4:5

5 Get wisdom, get understanding; do not forget my words or turn away from them.

It was a wet and rainy Friday night, the night before Sabreena and Aaron's scheduled wedding day. Evelyn sat with Sabreena, who was staring at the unopened envelope. "So, you've had this letter all these days and never even opened it? Sabreena, this is your life. The answers that decide which direction that your life is going in is enclosed in that envelope. So please, tell me again why I'm here and why you haven't read Aaron's letter", Evelyn questioned.

Sabreena responded emotionally, "I can't do it Sissy. I just couldn't bring myself to open it. I'm so afraid that I'll read it and hate him forever. I don't know if what he's trying to tell me will make it better or worse. So, I need you to open it and read it. Nobody in this world knows me better than you Eve. You have to do this for me. I don't even need to know what's in the letter. Just read it and tell me if it justifies me forgiving Aaron and going through with this wedding, or if I should just move on with my life and never look back".

Evelyn listened intently before she replied, "Bree, I will read the letter, but I will not make one of the most important decisions of your life for you. Give me the letter. I will sit and read it in silence and then we will talk". Sabreena handed the sealed envelope over to her sister. Evelyn opened it and began to read it. Tears began to roll down her face as she read in silence. Sabreena couldn't stand still. So many thoughts ran rapid through her mind. She began to pace back and forth as Evelyn flipped the pages of the letter.

Evelyn finished reading, folded the letter and placed it back into the envelope. She was hit with an overwhelming wave of emotions, and she could no longer hold it back. She dropped to her knees and began sobbing like she'd gotten news of someone's death. Sabreena, who was already unraveling emotionally, began to panic. "Eve, what's wrong? Oh My God it's really that bad", Sabreena exclaimed as she dropped to the floor to embrace Evelyn. Sabreena began to sob as herd as her sister. "It's ok. I don't need to know. I don't want to know. I'm making my decision. The wedding is off".

"No!", Evelyn shouted as she broke away from Sabreena's embrace and sprang to her feet. Sabreena, clearly confused now, questioned, "Why Sissy? I don't understand. You're so upset. It has to be something unforgiveable". Evelyn wiped the tears from her face and took a seat on the sofa as she regained her composure. Once she felt she had gotten herself together, she spoke to Sabreena in a soft and heartfelt voice, "Bree. You don't understand. Sit down and listen closely. I need to explain some things to you, and I pray you will fully understand once I'm done".

Sabreena sat down next to Evelyn, and they held hands. Evelyn took a deep cleansing breath and began to explain, "Bree, you have to keep an open mind, because what I'm about to share with you will oppose everything you ever thought to be true as far as reality is concerned. When I was in that coma, I went somewhere else. I was aware of everything happening in that hospital room, yet I was somewhere else. It was bright and calm and peaceful where I was. I thought I was dead. I thought I'd died and gone to heaven. I rested in this place for a bit before I started communicating with something. I never used my voice, I just thought things, and something answered every question or explained things extensively to me without me ever even seeing an actual being. I felt its presence and I knew it meant me well, so I had no fear. I asked if I was dead, and it responded telepathically to me that I was just resting in a safe place until my body was stronger and rejuvenated. After it made that clear to me, I was shown different parts of my life and made known why things happened the way they did. I was reminded that this was all Divinely orchestrated and that we were never alone or forsaken by what is known there as Source Energy. Here we say God in many different languages. Bree, I was reminded that I contracted my life to a Divine purpose and that my experience with Troy was no accident. There's a such thing as soul contracts and soul ties. I'd been shown that Troy was a Karmic soul contract that had to be fulfilled. He was what's known as a False Twin Flame. I later stumbled across while looking for answers, sitting in that hospital bed. I found them in a book called, "Twin Flames & The Event, by Jen McCarty". It explained why I could never just cut him loose no matter what we'd gone through. I now know that only upon his physical death, could my heart and soul free him from me, and our soul tie contract be completed. Again, this was all fated. It was then communicated that I would wake up from that tragic event different from what remembered before my near-death experience. I was told that this would all lead to me coming into union with my true twin flame counterpart in this lifetime. Bree, these Twin Flame connections are not just for the sake of being in union with your person. They have a bigger purpose. They're meant to awaken each other to our higher selves and our purpose, both separately and as a couple in union. These connections are sacred to the Most High God because they create Divine orchestrated change on a universal level. They place us in alignment to carry out our parts together in God's plan for humanity. I know it all sounds a bit sci-fi, but it's all true. Everything that we go through in this life is preparation and proof of us being ready to receive access to our spiritual gifts, come into successful union with our twin, and fulfill our soul purpose contracts. Everything that looked like attacks on our lives were actually practice, teachings and strengthening for whatever it is that we came to do.

Before I woke up in that hospital room, I was shown that I would have access to my spiritual gifts. Gifts that I was unaware of before that tragic event. Gifts that this event was a catalyst for unlocking. Bree, I had so many questions after that was revealed to me; but before I could get them answered, I was awake and in handcuffs in that hospital bed".

Evelyn took a pause from explaining. She looked at her sister to get a read on whether this was all too much or too farfetched for Sabreena to take in. She realized that there was no resistance in her sister's energy, so she continued to explain, "Bree, our lives have never been simple or easy, but we've always found a way to be ok. I've now been experiencing visions and clairaudient communication. I am still learning how to tap into these gifts at will, but for the most part things are just happening sporadically. Sometimes I'm afraid that I'll miss a warning, or a message and bad things will happen because of it. I felt so overwhelmed with guilt about Marie being murdered, but it wasn't until just reading Troy's letter that I was given Divine clarity. Bree, listen to me. I now am clear on two things: Felix is my person, the true other half of my soul; and Aaron is yours. You don't have to believe me or any of this for that matter. I now see that God shows us

what we need to see, all in Divine timing.
While I hope this is your time to wake up to
this, I am not in control of it. I'm merely a
messenger. I know I've just dumped a lot
on you, and you have so much to digest and
think about. So, I'm going to leave this
letter with you and suggest that you read it
with Christ like compassion, and then make
your decision. Felix will send me back here
by 4pm tomorrow afternoon through his car
service. Whether you'll be dressed for a
wedding or asking me to sit with you while
you cry it out over a bottle of wine is up to
you. But nonetheless, I will be here in
support of your decision, like I always am
baby sis".

Evelyn handed Sabreena the letter
back and grabbed her things. She strongly
embraced her little sister, feeling as if an
entire world was lifted from her shoulders.
She gave her a glance of admiration and
love before turning and walking out of
Sabreena's door. Sabreena was already
blown away at what her sister had just
confided in her. Now, her heart pounded
with anxiety at what was in the envelope.
She poured herself a large glass of red wine
and sipped on it until she felt relaxed. She
said a silent prayer before opening the

folded pages, then she read the contents of the letter.

Sabreena could not help but to cry uncontrollably as she learned what she was not aware of before. She read the letter in its entirety and wept as she replayed her and Evelyn's conversation, her relationship's ups and downs with Aaron, and now the contents of that letter. Sabreena was too overwhelmed with thought and emotions to even begin thinking of the rest of her life in that moment. She just felt as if her whole world had changed in just an hour's time. She finished her glass of wine, grabbed the throw blanket from the back of her couch, curled up with a pillow and gently cried herself to sleep.

Romans 12:12

12 Be joyful in hope, patient in affliction, faithful in prayer.

Sabreena jumped up, startled by the sound of her doorbell ringing at seven in the morning. It had been so long since she booked the glam squad to do her hair, make-up, and nails in her home for the wedding. With all that was happening, she totally forgot that she never canceled them. She hesitated for a moment and then decided to take it as a sign of good faith that everything was happening as it was meant to. Sabreena apologized for not being showered and ready for her services. She let the team in to set up their stations and she sprinted for a quick shower.

The team wasted no time getting to work to prepare Sabreena for her special day. She was making good time. She knew Evelyn would be there promptly at 4pm. Her ceremony was scheduled for that evening at 8pm in Felix's formal event room. It was private and had a small guest list of immediate family and close friends. Sabreena knew she still had to get touch ups and get changed into her gown at Felix's, so she made sure she was going to be ready when the car service arrived. At 3:30 pm she gathered her touch-up kit and her wallet and made sure it was in her oversized tote with the rest of her necessities.

Sabreena was on schedule for once. "Well, this must be a good sign because I'm never on time", Sabreena said aloud to herself. She was waiting out front for Evelyn to pull up and she had ten minutes to spare. "I got time to grab me some Starbucks on the way. Oh, and I got a gift card too", Sabreena thought to herself. She sat her things neatly on her steps and ran upstairs to search for that gift card that she'd forgot to use repeatedly. Her previously tidy room looked ransacked once she finished looking for her gift card, but she found it. "Yup, today is going to be perfect. I can feel it", Sabreena said as she made her way back down the stairs and to the front door with just a couple of minutes to spare.

The car pulled up a couple of minutes later and Evelyn jumped out and embraced Sabreena, jumping up and down with joy. "Yes God, we're having a wedding today! I'll call Felix and let him know that I'm on the way with the bride to be! I'm so excited Bree", Evelyn shouted joyfully. "Wait sissy, I haven't talked to Aaron yet. I just wanted it to be a surprise",

Sabreena replied. "Ok, I'll just shoot him a text and tell him to keep it under wraps", Evelyn responded. Sabreena requested that they stop at the nearby Starbucks. The driver complied. ***"Making a pitstop and then we will be on our way"***, Evelyn texted Felix to update him.

"Ma'am, your total is $15.75 today", a voice said from the drive through speaker. Sabreena reached for her tote to get her change purse so that she could add the $0.75 to the fifteen-dollar gift card. "Where the heck is my wallet? I know I tossed it on the top", Sabreena said as she fished through the massive tote. "Girl, here. That thing probably traveled to the bottom while you were carrying it", Evelyn said while handing Sabreena a $1.00 bill. "Thanks sissy, it better be in there though. My License and my favorite eyeliner are in there", Sabreena said thankfully. "Girl, you are so much like Marie that it's scary sometimes. Worried about your license and your eyeliner like your face isn't beat to perfection and like you'll be driving today", Evelyn teased.

Evelyn and Sabreena sang and danced in their seats, just enjoying the ride and in great spirits about the evening ahead. As they started crossing a bridge, their private celebration was interrupted by a hard bump to the rear of the vehicle. "What the hell?!", Sabreena said in a panic. As they turned back to see what was happening, they saw a black van coming full speed at them. Before they could even brace for the impact, the van plowed into them and both drivers, the driver of the van and their driver lost control and they both went flying over the side of the bridge and into the river.

The impact knocked everyone unconscious, and onlookers watched as both vehicles hit the water and sank slowly with no signs of survivors exiting the vehicles. People began calling for help and the bystanders that were on jet skis and in boats were jumping into the water without thought to render some assistance. Sirens from the water rescue teams could be heard from afar. Pure chaos surrounded the vehicles as they became further and further submerged by the body of water. Water rescue arrived and demanded that the helping Samaritans clear out and let them work. An onlooker from a nearby boat recorded the scene as they watched divers jumping into the water. "I don't think anyone survived this. This is so sad", a bystander stated as they watched in terror. It didn't look promising.

Within minutes, divers began reaching the surface with bodies, but no one could see whether they were dead or alive. They just witnessed the bodies being placed on water stretchers and assigned to rescue rigs and then watched as each rig sped away. Each time onlookers watched in hopes to see some signs of life and four times over, there were none. Everyone was pulled from the wreckage, yet no one watching knew if any of them had survived. There was a blanket of sadness that seemed to come over the bystanders as they watched the sunken cars and debris be cleared from the water. Lights and sirens soon faded away and the scene was overrun by news crews and reporters trying to put the pieces of this tragedy together.

Romans 12:12

*Be joyful in hope, patient in
affliction, faithful in prayer.*

The live band played in the
background as Felix tried calming Aaron's
nerves while phoning Evelyn repeatedly in
between. "Felix, give it up Bro! She's not
coming. She made up her mind. I just need
to accept it! You know how they are.
Evelyn is not going to answer. Those
women stick together. They're probably on
their way to Mexico with your driver,
blasting Beyonce and headed to celebrate
the "Best Thing I Never Had". Daniel has
called Bree just as many times as you've
called Eve. If they're ignoring his calls,
then you know we don't stand a chance. I
just gotta chalk this one man", Aaron
pleaded frantically.

Felix had another concern. He
couldn't get a hold of his driver by phone or
through dispatch. He knew something was
wrong, but he wanted to remain calm until
he got some answers. Especially since
Aaron was already falling apart. He had his
assistant working on getting those answers
as he continued to try and reach Evelyn and
keep Aaron together. However, he was

growing very close to losing his cool himself.

He was sitting in the area reserved for the reception when his assistant signaled for him to come. He had the wait staff pour Aaron a drink to keep him calm and he told Aaron to sit tight while he went to see what information his assistant had for him. As Felix made his way towards his assistant, Aaron watched to make sure he was far away to not interfere with what he was about to do. Aaron made his way over to the DJ and grabbed a microphone. "Attention ladies and gentlemen, family and friends. I just want to thank you all for coming out to witness the biggest day of my life as well as to celebrate Sabreena and me. Unfortunately, as you can all see, there is no Sabreena", Aaron stated sadly. Felix was dealing with something that required his immediate attention, so he frustratedly allowed Aaron to continue with his premature announcement while he spoke with a representative of the local police.

The wedding guests whispered and gasped as Aaron spoke. "Please feel free to make your way over to your assigned tables so that the staff can serve you dinner and drinks. I would like for you to at least enjoy yourselves tonight. It's the least I can do for you all since I've mistakenly wasted everyone's time. If any of you have left gifts in the designated gift drop off area, I'd understand fully if you went to retrieve them whenever you all leave. Again, thank you for coming out tonight and my deepest and most humble apologies for the inconvenience", Aaron speedily finished his apologetic speech as he saw Felix rushing in towards him.

"Aaron let's go. Come with me and I'll fill you in once we're in the car", Felix stated firmly. Aaron could see the intensity on Felix's face, and he began to worry. "What is it, Felix? Are they okay? You're scaring me bro", Aaron stated as Felix's speed seemed to pick up to a light sprint towards the awaiting car. The two of them got in and Felix broke down as they were pulling off. "Talk to me Felix! Please man. I need to know that they're at least okay. Felix, talk to me man! I just need to know they're ok", Aaron repeated frantically. "I don't know! Oh, God! Please help me", Felix cried out with his head held in his hands as he wept in fear. "What do you mean bro? What's happening? Where are we going? Felix what the hell did you find out man? I need to know what's happening", Aaron cried out in a panic.

Felix pulled himself together enough to explain. "They located the car. It was run off of a bridge by a van. Everyone went into the water. They won't tell me much more except that they retrieved my car in the wreckage and that we need to meet with the detective handling the wreck", Felix explained through teary eyes before he was interrupted by Aaron. "Wha... What? Is this some sick joke?! Wreck? Detective? Why is there a detective? Are they dead? Oh God Please, this can't be real. Felix, just say they're all alive", Aaron cried in response to being filled in.

The two of them spent the rest of the ride, anxiously waiting to be updated on the status of their women and Felix's driver. Holding back tears as best as possible, they remained quiet and full of fear and questions until reaching detective headquarters. When they arrived, they were escorted into a private conference room. The two of them were over the top with emotion as they waited for the investigating detective to join them. The detective entered the room and established the relationship between Aaron, Felix and the victims of his case. Once he established that, he began to fill them in on the details. "We have three victims who nearly drowned and are in intensive care. We have one victim who was deceased on arrival. She never made it out of the water alive. We were able to identify everyone except one of the victims in the ICU", the detective began. He turned to Aaron with a look of sorrow in his eyes as he continued. "Aaron, I'm sorry but the DOA victim was identified at the scene as Sabreena Williams. You will have to identify her body so that we can finish processing her as the deceased. I need to warn you that her face is pretty beat up and swollen from the impact of the accident", the detective explained.

Aaron stood up in reaction to the news, but immediately fell into the conference table as if the life just left his body. Felix reached out and grabbed him as his limp body went crashing into the table. "I'll give you two some time to process this", the detective said as he left the room. "She's gone! My angel. She's gone! What kind of God would take her away from me... from all of us?! How is she just...gone?! I don't want to take another breath if she can't bro! I don't want to be here! I can't be here. I can't do life without

her! I won't! I won't", Aaron shouted out
in emotional grief.

Aaron's emotional rant was
interrupted by his phone ringing repeatedly.
"Oh my God. It's Daniel! We left him and
didn't tell him anything. I can't tell him
this. It's going to kill him. Man, Eve is in
that hospital unconscious and not knowing
what's happening. This is going to destroy
us all! I can't do this bro. I can't do it",
Aaron said panicking once again. Felix just
sat in a daze, trying to take it all in without
falling apart too.

After collecting his thoughts, he
dialed Daniel himself. "D? Hey bro. I'm
going to have one of my cars bring you to us
and we will explain what's- -", Felix was
explaining before he was interrupted by
Daniel. "I'm already in a car. The hospital
called and said that they had Evelyn there.
I'm her next of kin, so they called me. I still
can't reach Bree though. I wanted her to
meet me there. She'll fall apart if she's by
herself and she has to see Eve in a hospital
bed again. I was just wondering if she's
answered Aaron's call yet, because her
phone is going straight to voicemail every
time I try to call her", Aaron rattled on.

Felix hesitated before responding, "No, she hasn't answered. Me and Aaron will just meet you at the hospital". The detective came in and explained the rest of the process. "It can wait. I need to support my family at the hospital right now. Besides, her brother needs to be caught up and included in this process", Aaron explained to the detective before he and Felix parted ways with the detective and headed to the hospital.

Aaron and Felix arrived at the hospital to find Daniel already bedside with Evelyn. His face was swollen and soaked with tears. They pulled up chairs next to Evelyn. Felix placed her dainty hand in his and rested his head on her legs and began to sob. Aaron cried silently, not just at the thought of losing Sabreena, but also at the thought of having to inform Daniel of her sudden and unfortunate death.

The three of them sat in silence, each praying at different times in their mind for God to make the best of what was to come from this tragedy. Daniel thought back to Evelyn being in a coma and then his thoughts rapidly went to Sabreena. "I'm so angry with Bree! Who is so stubborn and prideful that they would turn their phone off just because they decided they wanted to be a runaway bride? I don't understand it. Wasn't Eve on her way to her? Did she refuse to be reasonable and go through with the ceremony? What happened between the two of them that she would turn her phone off when Eve left her? I mean, I get that Eve probably dug into her about her having everyone show up for a wedding ceremony that she had no plans on going through with...Sorry Aaron, but I'm just trying to understand her logic right now. Sissy needs her here and she's somewhere being a self-entitled brat!", Daniel went on in a tangent before his outburst was met with a shrieking cry from Aaron.

"Stop! Please. I can't do this! Please stop talking about her that way", Aaron cried out before hopping up out of the chair. The force from him standing so quickly knocked the chair over backwards and he left the room in a hurry. You could hear his cries all the way down the hall as he made his way to a nearby restroom to get himself together. As he turned the corner, he heard a familiar voice off in the distance.

"I just want to know why I am waking up in cuffs officer. I don't even remember how I got here or what happened to me. Please help me understand what I could have done to get myself here", the voice said pleading to someone in one of the ICU rooms. Aaron stood frozen in his tracks just listening. "Ma'am. Witnesses observed you running another vehicle off of the road and into the river today. You lost control and went in behind them. Two people are badly injured, and one is dead. The witnesses seem to think it was intentional. Listen, I'm just doing my job. I'm sure the proper authorities will come and speak to you", the officer replied.

Aaron was overcome by a rush of emotions as he ran towards the room. "Are you serious? My crazy Ex is behind all of this?", he thought to himself as he quickly approached the room's doorway. When he got close enough to the door, the officer seated outside of the room jumped up to stop Aaron from entering. "I'm sorry sir. This patient can't have visitors. I don't know who let you up here but – ", the officer said but was abruptly cut off by Aaron. "I need to see her! You don't understand. I gotta just see", Aaron was saying hysterically before he was interrupted. A voice shouted from the room saying, "Aaron? Is that you?". Aaron could no longer withstand the confusion and emotional chaos and his body gave way. He passed out on the spot.

"Please, take these cuffs off of me. I need to get out of here. I'm scared and so confused. Someone please, help me understand what's happening", the woman yelled. All of the commotion drew the medical staff and the other visitors' attention to the entrance of the room. The nursing staff rushed in to help Aaron, who had fallen right into the officer's arms and was placed gently on the floor.

Felix and Daniel, who also heard all of the commotion, made their way towards all of the excitement only to see Aaron stretched out on the floor with hospital staff and a police officer standing over him. "What the hell?!", Felix spouted as he high tailed it towards Aaron. "Officer, I'm his attorney. What's going on. Did you do something to him?", Felix asked in an effort to clear up some of this confusion.

The officer responded, "Stand back please. He's not in any trouble. He wanted to enter the room. I'm not sure why. But something upset him so badly that I literally watched his eyes roll back and he fell forward into my arms. I placed him on the floor, so he's not hurt in any way. The staff is trying to figure out what's going on with him. We need to stand back and let them work", the officer explained.

With everything happening so fast, neither Felix nor Daniel was tuned in to the commotion going on inside of the ICU room. "What the hell?! Bree?! Is that you in there", Daniel said in confusion. "D! Yes, it's me. Please bro. I'm so scared. These cops are saying I ran someone off the road. I don't remember. I don't want to be here. Where's Eve? I thought I heard Aaron's voice. Is he with you?", Sabreena cried out from the hospital room. "Officer, please get me someone in charge. I believe there's been a huge mistake", Felix began explaining.

Aaron slowly came to and remembered hearing Sabreena's voice before collapsing. "She's not dead. I heard her voice. Please let me see who is in that room", Aaron shouted at everyone standing around. "We got you bro. It's ok. Yes, Sabreena is ok and very much alive. She is still confused a bit due to the impact from the accident, but I am waiting for the detective to arrive so that we can clear this all up", Felix explained. Daniel, who was still way outside of the loop instantly lost his cool. "What the hell is going on? Why would you think she was dead? What am I missing? Don't everyone speak up at once", Daniel ranted in anger and confusion.

"Listen, we have caused enough disruption on a floor that we're supposed to be super quiet on. Let's find a nearby conference room and I will explain everything to you and then we can wait there for the detective, so that we can clear the rest of this mess up", Felix replied calmly. The guys made their way to the conference room. Daniel held it together while Felix and Aaron filled him in. The detective had impeccable timing, because he entered the conference room just as Daniel was all caught up.

He sat the family down and explained. "Sabreena's ID was found inside of the pocket of the deceased body. Her face was battered and swollen from the collision, so we just assumed that it was Sabreena Williams. Sabreena, whose face was also pretty battered and swollen, was the only person who did not have any ID, so we labeled her as Jane Doe and the driver of the van. We had no way of knowing which vehicle either of them came from because they were both in the water and completely freed from the vehicles. Evelyn and the driver were the only two people who were seat belted in and still inside the vehicle when they were rescued.

If it weren't for the positioning of the car, there wouldn't have been a large air pocket in the top of the vehicle and both Evelyn and the driver may have drowned while trapped inside. A bystander on a jet ski actually pulled Sabreena up by the arm and held onto her unconscious body until rescue arrived within minutes. The other woman who is in our morgue was not so lucky. The divers pulled her out and she was unable to be resuscitated. We are just putting two and two together and learning that the deceased woman is the wanted suspect in Marie Williams murder and the woman behind all of the stalking of your family. Aaron, we still need you to come down to the morgue and give us a positive ID on her. The only thing we haven't figured out is how she got a hold of Sabreena's ID. We are hoping Sabreena can help us with that once she is feeling a little better", the detective explained in detail.

"So, you two thought my baby sister was dead and didn't think to mention it to me? You left Felix's house without even saying two words to me! How is it that MY sisters were involved in all of this mess, but NOBODY thought to say a word to me?! That is fowl! I am beyond pissed", Daniel spat off. "We can't say sorry enough. It wasn't like that D. We both panicked and before we knew it, it was like our worlds came crashing down and time stood still all at the same time. When I realized we had left you out of the loop, I was both distraught and terrified of telling you what was going on. I was so traumatized bro. Please, don't charge this to our hearts. Our heads were somewhere else. I don't even know what else to say because sorry isn't enough and I know this. But I'm really sorry bro", Aaron said apologetically.

Felix shook his head in agreement, waiting on a response from Daniel. "I'm just glad they're both alive. I can't lose either of them. Life has been crazy for us but being here together is the only way that we've managed to be remotely ok. I'm still plenty pissed, but I personally know how these things can take us out of our sensible train of thought", Daniel said with a forgiving tone. The detective wrapped up the briefing with the family, then escorted them to Sabreena's room. The cuffs were now removed, and Sabreena became overwhelmed with emotion just at the sight of them entering her hospital room.

Daniel attempted to make his way over to embrace his sister but was nearly knocked over by Aaron rushing in to get to Sabreena. "Yeah. You gotta give him this one bro. They've been apart for weeks and then he thought her for dead just a few hours ago. He may not even let her go today. I'm just saying", Felix teased as he and Daniel both laughed in unison.

Daniel's phone started ringing, just as Aaron stepped aside to make room for Daniel to hug Sabreena. He leaned in and hugged her with tears of joy streaming down his face. His long embrace was interrupted by his phone ringing again. "You got a girlfriend that you ain't telling me about or something", Sabreena asked intrusively. Daniel, shaking his head and laughing at her question answered, "No baby sis. I don't recognize the number, so I wasn't going to answer. I guess I better answer, since they're calling me back... Hello?", Daniel said as he answered, and his face lit up at the sound of the voice on the other end. "Sissy! You're awake! Oh, Allah is merciful! Thank you! Thank you", Daniel blurted out at the sound of hearing Evelyn up and aware. He explained that he was just around the hall with Sabreena and that he and Felix would be there shortly.

He hung up and was confused at how hard Sabreena was laughing. "What's so funny sis", Daniel asked. Sabreena replied while still laughing, "Boy... Felix cut outta this room as soon as he realized you were talking to Eve. You were praising Allah and he was out the door and running through the halls like a mad man. He was not waiting for you. He got it bad". The three of them laughed in unison at Felix rushing to Evelyn with not so much as a peep to anyone.

"I guess I will give those two their time. I'm starting to feel like the third wheel no matter which way I turn", Daniel said with a little sadness in his voice. Sabreena rolled her eyes and spat back, "Oh shut up you big baby. You can be the front wheel to our tricycle any day. I love you, big brother! I'm just happy that this day didn't end with me in the body bag that the officers had me lined up for and...Oh My God! Aaron, what about our wedding? Does anyone know where we are or what happened?", Sabreena said in a panic after the realization that she was indeed enroute to her big day when this all happened.

"Hey hey hey. Relax angel face. You just get better. Felix and I are handling everything. Besides, you can't marry anyone looking like you just had a fight with Tommy Hearns and lost", Aaron said playfully. "Too soon Aaron. Do I really look that bad babe", Sabreena asked in a whining tone. "My beautiful brown angel, just you being alive and able to look at me with those beautiful eyes is a blessing from God. I don't care about any bruises and swelling. I love the soul of you. Nothing else will ever matter", Aaron said as he leaned in to kiss Sabreena's bruised and puffy face.

"Oh gosh. I'm gonna be sick! Yup! That's my Que. I'm outta here. Gonna go kiss Eve goodbye and leave all of the lovebirds to… I don't know. To do whatever lovebirds do", Daniel said as he got up and marched himself out Sabreena's hospital room. "See ya later hater", Sabreena chimed playfully as Daniel left. Daniel rushed to lay his eyes on Evelyn, and he said his goodbyes to her shortly after. He was famished, so he planned to catch his favorite Halal restaurant before they closed.

Daniel was nearing the elevator doors as they began to close. "Hey! Can you hold the door please", Daniel shouted as he began to jog towards the closing elevator doors, hoping that whoever was inside would hear him and keep the doors from closing. Just then, a dainty little hand appeared and waved the doors back open. Daniel stopped in his tracks just short of entering the elevator. "Well, are you getting on or not", the woman said, confused at Daniel's sudden stop in his stride, yet adorning a pleasant smile.

"Huh? Oh. Yes. My apologies. As salaam alaikum Sister. Please forgive me", Daniel replied nervously. "Oh, no worries, and wa alaikum assalam", the woman relied pleasantly. Daniel did his very best to not stare at the woman who was dressed in a hijab and overgarment. However, this was a difficult task. She had the most beautiful cocoa brown skin, vibrant almond shaped light brown eyes, the cutest button nose and small but plump kissable lips. But in some way, he felt that it was more than just her looks. She had a pleasant calmness about her that just radiated outwardly.

As the elevator doors opened to the lobby, Daniel's heart raced. The woman walked out before him, and he trotted slowly behind. His mind was so jumbled. He wanted to say something more before she got away from him. Nothing came to mind, so he just took to the pavement silently, standing within feet from her. Daniel stared at his phone, waiting for his rideshare service to pull up. He was a bit frustrated at the fact that his mouth literally would not open to say a word, despite the intense urge to speak up.

As Daniel's ride pulled up, he moved in front of the woman and stepped off the curb to open the door. "Shukran", The woman said softly while smiling. Daniel looked very confused. "Oh. Afwan... I think. I apologize. I thought this was my ride. Not that I wouldn't have opened the door for you. I would. I'm sorry to hold you up. I was just a little confused because I don't see another car and this one is showing on my app as being the car that they sent for me", Daniel replied nervously.

The woman, now confused, looked down at her phone and replied, "Oh. Maybe this is your ride. Let me be sure. I apologize. I may have moved too fast without paying attention because I'm trying to get a bite to eat from my favorite Halal restaurant before it closes".

Just then, the driver realized the reason behind all of the confusion, and he spoke up. "Ma'am. Sir. I think I'm here for the both of you. You both selected a shared ride for a cheaper fare. It just so happens that you both are being picked up and dropped off at the same location. If it's ok with the two of you, can you both get in so that we can be on our way? I have other fares to pick up after you", The driver said impatiently.

"Wow, he's so rude", the woman whispered to Daniel. "Yeah. He gets a one-star rating from me when this ride is over", Daniel replied as they both chuckled lightly. Fifteen minutes later, the driver pulled up to Al-Salam Grill at 924 Levick Street in Northeast Philadelphia. It was a quaint little Halal spot that was owned by the Halal meat market right next door to it. "This place has the most tender and perfectly cooked lamb chops. They own the halal meat market next door as well, so the food here is always fresh", the woman said excitedly to Daniel.

"Wow, I come here for the same exact thing. I'm sorry sister, I didn't ask your name", Daniel said inquisitively. "My name is Sadiqa. And Your name is?", the woman replied and questioned in return.

"My name is Daniel. I haven't chosen a
Muslim name and attribute yet sister. I'm
new to the faith and I am learning and
becoming more disciplined, but for some
reason I just don't feel that I am resonating
with any name in particular just yet", Daniel
replied. "It's ok brother. Allah knows your
heart", Sadiqa replied sweetly. "Indeed
Sister. Indeed", Daniel said. The two of
them opted to share a table and get further
acquainted.

They exchanged contact information
and Daniel waited until Sadiqa was in her
rideshare car before he called himself a ride.
As Daniel rode home, he thought about how
crazy the day had gone and he began to pray
silently. "Allah. You have a unique way of
blessing us. I am grateful for the experience
of it all. In some strange way, I'm
beginning to realize that there is a reason
behind all that we have endured. I know
only good can come of it, so I will always
wait in gratitude for the rainbow after the
storm. Ameen", Daniel said his short prayer
and ended his night in good spirits. He was
truly grateful for whatever was to come,
because for once, he truly believed that it
was all good.

Ephesians 3:16-19

16 I pray that out of his glorious riches he may strengthen you with power through his Spirit in your inner being, 17 so that Christ may dwell in your hearts through faith. And I pray that you, being rooted and established in love, 18 may have power, together with all the Lord's holy people, to grasp how wide and long and high and deep is the love of Christ, 19 and to know this love that surpasses knowledge—that you may be filled to the measure of all the fullness of God.

(Three Months Later)

"I can't believe we are all actually doing this. Never in my life have I been so impulsive. This is, by far, one of the craziest yet liberating things that I have ever done in my life. And I think that I'm a pretty adventurous guy if you ask me", Felix rattled on. "Well, nobody asked you. It's too hot and too early for all of your babbling", Sabreena said in a funk. "Bree, be nice. We are in India, it's beautiful here, we are alive and well. Life is good my friend", Sadiqa said very pleasantly. Sabreena cut her eyes over at Sadiqa, who pretended not to feel the daggering stares. "Easy newbie! I like you a lot, but let's not forget that it was you that pitched this crazy idea to all of us in the first place. So just understand that if I'm irritated about anything while we are here, it's automatically your fault Sadiqa", Sabreena retorted.

Sadiqa smiled nervously as she latched on to Daniel's arm for comfort. The six of them stood out in the heat waiting for their car service after their long flight. They had arrived in Calcutta as planned and were on schedule for their special evening. Felix and Evelyn found a seat in a shaded corner. Daniel and Sadiqa were so consumed in each other that the heat did not seem to bother them at all. Aaron rubbed his head anxiously as Sabreena whined about being tired and uncomfortable. "Yup, everything is exactly as I imagined so far", Evelyn said as she took notice of everyone's actions and whereabouts. Felix laughed quietly, because he understood exactly what she meant.

Their driver pulled up a few minutes later. Felix handed them a card with their intended destination that read, "*ama Stays & Trails 25 Farm House, Vedic Village, Kolkata*". The driver shook his head in the affirmative and began loading their belongings. The ride was peaceful and quiet as they all took notice of the beautiful sights through the windows. No one said it, but there was a different kind of peace that overtook them all as they made their way to their villa. While it was noticeably out of the ordinary to all of them, it was extremely comforting, and it showed in everyone's solemn appearance.

Time was of the essence once they arrived. The women retreated together to one of the rooms to get primped and pressed for their evening. The men scattered to other rooms to do the same. Evelyn handed Felix the itinerary with the evening's destination address, as they planned for the men to leave before them in a separate car and await their arrival. "I'm feeling so anxious babe. The last time you and Bree got into a car together to meet Aaron and I, we almost lost the two of you", Felix said.

Evelyn placed a single finger over Felix's lips to hush him. She pulled him in for a hug and just held onto him in silence, feeding him her tranquil energy until she heard his heartbeat slow to a steady and relaxed pace. She pulled herself away and just stared into Felix's eyes. Without using any words, she communicated to him that all was well and to remain at peace and in good thoughts. Felix's return gaze gave Evelyn confirmation that he received every bit of comfort and instruction that she was silently communicating. Feeling back at peace, Felix turned away from Evelyn and joined the guys in getting ready for the evening.

A little while later, the guys were all dressed and ready to go. "Ladies! The fellas are leaving the building. Don't keep us waiting too long", Daniel shouted out to Sadiqa and his sisters as he was headed out to the car with Felix and Aaron. "We won't", Sadiqa shouted in response from one of the rooms. With that, the guys were on their way to await their women, who were currently helping each other put the finishing touches on themselves. The three of them were so beautiful inside and out, each in their own way. Evelyn looked at herself in the mirror and then caught a glimpse of Sabreena and Sadiqa behind her. "Come on y'all. We've taken enough selfies. Let's get a few group photos, because we look goodt", Evelyn said proudly.

They snapped a few photos, some serious and some silly, before wrapping it up. "Ok, let's get out of here. We don't want to keep our men waiting", Sadiqa said.

"Girl hush! Ain't nobody thinking about us. I know Aaron needs a few minutes to himself. All I did was complain, the last few days. Truth is, I was so nervous about all of this, so I was being difficult. Aaron is so patient with me. He knew why I was behaving that way. I owe him an apology. But if I'm being honest, I'm glad y'all talked me into doing this. I think I needed it. Ooookay! I'm getting emotional. That's enough. Let's go", Sabreena said as she snapped out of her emotional state.

The three of them worked together to tidy up the space. "Hey, does anyone have their itinerary? I gave ours to Felix. I can't pronounce the name of the place, let alone remember it. I just want to hand it to the driver so that he knows where we are going", Evelyn said. Sabreena began searching for her itinerary. "I sat mine down in here somewhere. I know it was near my purse. I just need to shift some things around to see where exactly I left my purse. Then maybe… then maybe… maybe I can", Sabreena said as she began to break a sweat and stumble over her words.

Evelyn sensed something was off, so she turned her attention to Sabreena. "Bree! Bree what's wrong?!", Evelyn shouted in a panic as she rushed over to Sabreena. Sabreena was clutching her chest and gasping for air. Sadiqa ran to the other side of Sabreena to assist Evelyn in sitting her down. "I… I can't. Eve… I can't breathe", Sabreena panted through struggling breaths. Sadiqa began fanning Sabreena to give her added air. "Look at me baby sis. Feel my energy. Take a deep breath, in through your nose and blow it out slowly through your mouth. Come on Bree. You got this. Just Breathe with me. In and out. In and out. In and out. Ok, yes. There you go baby girl. Nice and slow", Evelyn said as she coached Sabreena through each breath.

Evelyn sat and watched as Sabreena regained her composure. Sabreena noticed a fluttered Sadiqa, sitting in a corner, still breathing the way Evelyn was just instructing. "What the hell are you doing over there Sadiqa", Sabreena spat. Evelyn, now becoming slightly annoyed at Sabreena, spoke out, "stop the nonsense, Sabreena Williams. Not this time. Leave Sadiqa alone. This is not about her. This moment is about you. So, let's have it". Sabreena knew exactly what her big sister was talking about. She rolled her eyes and sat silently.

Evelyn wasn't having any of it this time around. "You can roll your eyes until they fall out of your skull for all I care Bree, but we are having this conversation today! Right now!", Evelyn scolded. Sabreena gathered herself completely. "Sadiqa, do you mind leaving me and Eve to talk for a few minutes", Sabreena asked politely. Sadiqa nodded as she got up to leave the room. "What's going on Bree. Is this about you having doubts about Aaron or is this something else", Evelyn asked sternly.

"No, Aaron is the best. I can't see a life without him. I panicked. I couldn't find my purse. It was one of the last things I said before... before she ran us off the road. I couldn't find my wallet Eve. Next thing you know, my life was flashing before my eyes. I feel like a crazy person. Aaron was trying his best to reschedule the wedding and I kept giving him stupid excuses, all because everything is triggering me. I'm afraid to plan big events because I don't want anyone else to be shot or hurt or stalked. I freak out every time I can't find my purse. I'm falling apart and everyone else seems to be doing just fine after all of this", Sabreena explained emotionally.

Evelyn hugged Sabreena tight for a few seconds, then rested her forehead against Sabreena's for a few seconds more before sitting back and speaking. "Bree, we are all trying to get past this as best as we can. The difference is, Daniel and I seek comfort in our persons. We don't hide our emotions or our struggles from Felix and Sadiqa. Baby girl, that is why God has blessed us with such wonderful counterparts. You have to trust that Aaron can handle you even in your most vulnerable states. You would be there for him Bree. What makes you think that he doesn't feel the same way", Evelyn questioned.

"I'm afraid Sissy. I'm afraid that he will think I'm weak or that I'm burdensome and he will leave", Sabreena confessed. "Bree. That man loves you as much as he loves his own self. He didn't bathe for weeks when you cut him off. Felix said the stench in that home could walk around by itself when he found Aaron in there sulking. He can't function in life without you either silly. He loves you unconditionally. Hell, if you weren't my sister, I would've been cut you loose. You are a Royal pain in the Ass, but anyone who really knows you, knows that you have a heart of gold under that hard shell of yours", Evelyn said while chuckling.

Sabreena, now with tears rolling down her eyes, began to drop her head. Evelyn grabbed Sabreena gently by the chin and tilted her sister's head back up. "No ma'am. Chin up and head straight like the royalty that you are. Listen Bree. Needing someone is ok. We can't always do everything alone. Aaron loves you very deeply and it frustrates him when you don't allow him completely into your heart and soul. He has more than earned his place there Bree. I'm your big sister and I've been watching over you for the longest. It's time that I entrust someone else with that. I trust Aaron and it's time that you do too baby girl. He is more than worthy of that position. Open up to him Bree. It will begin to push him away after a while if he feels like nothing he does, or no amount of time makes you trust the love between the two of you. Baby girl, he is as real as it gets. He is your person. Now start showing him that you are his too", Evelyn advised lovingly.

The two of them leaned in for another hug. Sadiqa tapped gently at the door. "Hello in there. Is everything ok? The guys are texting me that they're worried", Sadiqa said from the other side of the door. "Yes, tell them we are leaving now. We are coming out now sis", Sabreena responded. Sadiqa smiled on the other side of the door. Sabreena called her sis. She felt that it was very endearing, since Sabreena always seemed so tough to her. Evelyn and Sabreena exited the room, and they all made their way to the car. Evelyn handed the driver the itinerary with a destination that read: ***Acharya Jagadish Chandra Bose Botanical Garden.*** The driver nodded and with that, they were off to meet the fellas.

They arrived at such a breathtaking sight. The three of them held hands while walking towards The Great Banyan Tree. It was more powerful of a sight than they all imagined. From the distance, it looked like a forest, but it was actually one great big tree with such big protruding roots that it looked like a bunch of trees. "Sadiqa, this is more beautiful than you described", Evelyn said in awe. When they got closer, they could see Felix, Daniel and Aaron all standing in their custom Indian made attire. They appeared to be standing in the middle of the forest with one other man who was dressed in all white authentic Indian garb.

Aaron, Felix and Daniel noticed their women approaching and all of their jaws dropped at such overwhelming beauty.

Sabreena had custom made Indian attire made to accentuate Aarons. They wore gold and black. Evelyn and Felix's attire was custom made to match as well in the colors of red gold and black. Daniel and Sadiqa followed suit, but their attire was closer to Muslim garb, matching a purple, silver and black theme. They all looked so perfect, standing under the banyan tree together. A professional photographer was making his way to them as they positioned themselves for their ceremonies. The official man dressed in white waited for them all to be standing comfortably with their counterparts before he started speaking.

He said a quick blessing over the three couples under The Great Banyan Tree before enlightening them all. He spoke saying, "*The banyan tree is considered as the symbol of immortality. It has aerial roots that grow down from its branches forming additional trunks and anchor the tree to the ground, therefore this tree is also known as Bahupada, or the one with several feet. This tree symbolizes the creator Brahma, as it symbolizes longevity. May the essence and symbolic nature of this tree bring the same blessings to your unions, in this life and the hereafter. Ase', Amen and Ameen*".

The Man dressed in all white officiated over the marital vows between each couple. Bystanders watched in admiration as each couple exchanged vows and rings. A professional photographer snapped photos, making sure to capture each intimate and delicate moment, shared between the couples. This was it: The momentous occasion that marked the ending of all their past traumatic karmic cycles and opened the door to their season of abundant harvest. Perfect union in God's sight, divinely ordered, guided, and carefully orchestrated. Three perfectly imperfect couples who traveled through such tumultuous trials and tribulations to reach such a perfect start to life. There they stood, under that banyan tree in all its great simplicity as the Official Man spoke these last words over all of them saying, "Here's to the start of your lives anew. May you write beautiful love stories together that awakens perfect and unconditional love, all around the world. The kind of love that sends healing ripples all throughout the Universe and beyond. All praises to The Most High Source of Creation. I raise my vibrations to you all, for this is just...

The Beginning!"

Ase'

Amen

And

Ameen

Made in the USA
Middletown, DE
28 October 2022